D1311657

Caught Up In A D-Boy's Illest Love 2

TN Jones

Caught Up In A D-Boy's Illest Love 2

Caught Up In A D-Boy's Illest Love 2 © 2017 by TN Jones.

All rights reserved. No part of this book may be reproduced in any form or by any electronic or mechanical means including information storage and retrieval systems, without permission in writing from the author. The only exception is by a reviewer, who may quote short excerpts in a review.

Cover designed by Bryant Sparks

This book is a work of fiction. Names, characters, places, and incidents either are products of the author's imagination or are used fictitiously. Any resemblance to actual persons, living or dead, events, or locales is entirely coincidental.

Acknowledgment

First, thanks must go out to the Higher Being for providing me with a sound body and mind; in addition to having the natural talent of writing and blessing me with the ability to tap into such an amazing part of life. Second, thanks most definitely go out to my Princess. Third, to my supporters and new readers for giving me a chance. Where in the world would I be without y'all?

Truth be told, I wouldn't have made it this far without anyone. I truly thank everyone for rocking with me. MUAH! Y'all make this writing journey enjoyable! I would like to thank everyone from the bottom of my heart for always rocking with the novelist kid from Alabama, no matter what I drop. Y'all have once again trusted me to provide y'all with quality entertainment.

Enjoy, my loves!

Caught Up In A D-Boy's Illest Love 2

TN Jones: Today, we will hear from Jonzella and Totta. I tried to have Dank and Jonsey come in as well, but they stated that they couldn't at this time. Totta and Jonzella, thank you for taking time out of your busy day to sit down with me.

Totta and Jonzella: You are welcome.

TN Jones: Jaw dropping information was revealed about you guys' relationship and personal life. How are things for you two?

Totta: Rocky, but nothing that we can't overcome.

Jonzella: For me, confusing, and like he said, rocky.

TN Jones: Tell us what is it like being in the center of chaos, lies, and treachery?

Jonzella: It's unexplainable. It's a place that I don't ever want to be in again. (Looks at Totta with a smirk on her face and a raised eyebrow)

TN Jones: In the first book, the readers and I didn't get a chance to know more about you. Will they in this book?

Both: Absolutely.

Totta: Y'all will get the good, bad, and the ugly from all of us. Each of us are faced with real issues that can potentially get us hurt and could possibly push those that we love away.

TN Jones: In book two, what will be revealed?

Totta: Fuckery. (shakes head while exhaling sharply)

Jonzella: A lot of disturbing shit that I'm still trying to understand. (phone begins to ring … excuses herself)

Caught Up In A D-Boy's Illest Love 2

TN Jones: Totta, do you see your— (cut off because of Jonzella's remark)

Jonzella: Don't you take yo' ass over that damn man's house, Jonsey. It's not wor—! Totta, we gotta go now!

Totta: Sorry, TN Jones, I think you need to tell the readers to flip the page to continue reading our story.

TN Jones: Welp, readers...I think you know what you need to do. Indulge on Casey, Totta, Jonsey, and Jonzella's story as it is told by them.

Chapter 1
Jonsey

Friday, January 13th, 2017

After we learned of who we had been sleeping with, Jonzella passed out as I held my breath, shaking my head, and praying that my parents were wrong. Shaking Jonzella awake, I had shocked facial expressions still plastered across my face while glaring into her eyes.

Our parents were talking as I mouthed to Jonzella, "Are you okay?" She nodded her head, but didn't make a single move.

My body felt queasy; thus, I dropped my head on the firm pillow. Our parents were so involved in their conversation that they didn't notice Jonzella, or I, were asking questions.

"Don't go asking around about these guys. Do you understand me, ladies?" our father stated sternly, bringing Jonzella and I out of zombie land.

"Yes, sir," we replied in unison.

"Call us before you go on y'all's trip. Make sure to have fun. By the way, who are y'all leaving with?" our mother inquired.

"Just us, Mom," Jonzella blurted out while looking at me.

"Phew. Great. Call us soon as y'all get on the road."

"We will. We love y'all," Jonzella and I stated in unison as we tried to sound as normal as possible.

After we ended the call, Jonzella crept out of my bed and closed and locked the door before turning around to face me with the 'oh shit' facial expression. My poor little behind was lying on the bed as if I was paralyzed. I didn't know what to think, say, or do.

Soon as she brought her body to my bed, pulled the covers back, and laid down, Jonzella spat in a low timbre, "We are fucking around with the guys that our brothers witnessed murder a man, Jonsey. What the fuck are we going to do? Totta's in the room sleep. Bitch, I'm scared to go in there. How do I get him out of here?"

"I don't know," I responded in a hushed tone.

"Oh, shit. Oh, shit. Oh, shit," she kept saying repeatedly as she covered her mouth, and tears began to slide down her oval-shaped face.

With a racing heartbeat, I mouthed, "What?"

"I showed Totta our family pictures of us in the Bahamas last summer, and I told him the names of our brothers and parents," she stated as she tried to hold back more tears.

"Oh my God, Jonzella," I responded as horrible thoughts crept into my mind.

"We have to get rid of them. They could hurt us. There is no doubt in my mind that they are using us, especially knowing that

Kevin and Kenny are our brothers. We must put some distance between us and them, Jonsey. I wouldn't—," she was cut off by Totta calling her pet name.

"My sweet queen, where are you?"

"I'm in here with Jonzella trying on clothes," she lied as she looked at me.

"Okay. Have y'all packed y'all's thousands of suitcases?" he laughed.

"Not yet," she replied as tears slid down her face.

"I'm headed to the house to grab a couple of items. I'll be back in a minute, okay?"

"Okay," she responded.

Silence.

"Are you mad at me or some, Jonzella?" he questioned oddly.

"No. Why would you ask me that?" her shaky voice asked.

"Come out of Jonsey's room and face me," Totta demanded.

Shaking her head while mouthing that she didn't want to, I mouthed to remain calm as she could.

"A'ight," she said as normal as she could before pulling the covers off her body.

By the time my sister was in front of the door, I was out of the bed and in my closet—throwing clothes on the ground as if we were actually trying them on. Soon as she opened the door, Totta roughly pulled her to him, and the gasp that came out of her mouth scared the shit out of me.

"Mane, what's wrong with you?" he inquired.

"Nothing," she lied.

"What I told you about lying to me, Jonzella? Do I lie to you?"

Silence.

"I asked you a question."

"I think we need some time apart," she blurted out.

Why in the fuck is you going to say that shit while he is here, nutbasket? I thought as I slid further into my closet.

"Jonzella, what in the hell are you talking about 'we need some time apart'?"

"We are moving too fast. Last night and earlier this morning got me thinking that we are moving waaayy too fast."

"You got to be shitting me, right?" he asked quizzically.

Silence.

"Answer me, damn it!" he yelled, which caused me to jump.

"Yes, I'm kidding. You are my Zaddy; why in the hell would I want to cease things between the two of us? I just wanted to see you get mad that's all. You know that shit be turning me on," she stated in her normal tone.

Lightly chuckling, he casually replied, "You play too much, my sweet queen. You know a nigga got mad feelings for you, right?"

"Yes. As I for you."

Before Totta left, they engaged in a passionate kiss. Soon as she locked the door behind him, she was running down the hallway into the bathroom. Hurling noises from her informed me what she was doing. Stepping away from the closet, I asked, "Are you okay?"

"Noooo!" she cried out before vomiting in the toilet.

"All of our windows are completely locked and sealed. They can't come in. Please tell me that Totta doesn't have a key to our crib, Jonzella," I asked seriously.

"No, he doesn't," she sadly responded as she flushed the toilet.

"Can I be honest?"

"Yes."

"I'm scared as hell. I don't know what to do or say."

"That makes two of us."

Walking out of the bathroom, I retreated to my bed. I was a ball of confusion. I wanted to know why this was happening to my sister and me. I had to know if this was a game that they were playing with us. The ways towards us were loving and caring.

Could the ultimate reason for being that was to play under us so that they could get our brothers? Are we as gullible as they think we are? Will they kill us also? What are we to do? How can we get rid of them? As questions flooded my mind, I rehashed past events of me pillow talking with Casey.

Sighing heavily as I felt dizzy, I wanted to believe that he would never harm me; however, I could never be sure with the current situation him and Totta were involved in. Fresh out of thoughts, I broke down and cried. I cried for my family, self, Casey, Totta, and Jonzella. As I cried, I heard Jonzella weeping as well. Our repeatedly ringing cell phones didn't cease us from crying.

For thirty minutes, we cried until the knocks sounded off at our front door, which neither of us answered. I stood still on my bed as I didn't know what in the world Jonzella was doing. I was too afraid to run in her room to see; in fear that either Totta or Casey would see me.

Chapter 2
Dank

"What took you so long answering the door, Ms. Lady?" Casey asked sweetly as he pulled me towards him.

As Totta waltzed passed us, in a joking manner, he said, "Her ass probably went back to sleep. She still looks like she got morning breath."

"Shut yo' ass up... snitching and shit," she stated while laughing, which was an odd type of chuckle.

Something's wrong with my queen. I hope she ain't tripping about that Diamond bullshit, I thought as she spoke.

"After we tried on clothes, I laid back down. I'm sorry; I'm not ready," she voiced lightly as she laid her head on my chest.

"That's okay. Totta and I will drive. You and Jonzella can sleep," I passionately told her before planting a kiss on her forehead.

Two hours and thirty minutes later, we hit the road. I told her to set her phone for a reason; so that we wouldn't be leaving out at two-thirty in the afternoon. All I could do was shake my head at them; hell, women in general. You give them a specific time to be ready, and their asses still won't be ready. On the road, the ladies were extremely quiet. That disturbed me a lot because normally, they would be laughing and joking.

"What is really up with y'all?" Totta finally asked, looking in the back seat.

"I'm saying. Any other time, y'all would be cutting up really bad. What got y'all's panties in a bunch?" I inquired as I jumped on I-65 South, heading towards Mobile.

"I'm tired," they spat in unison.

"Dope dick will do you that way," Totta joked.

Shaking my head, I chuckled while looking in the rearview mirror at my queen. Her face was the reason why I threw on the hazard lights and quickly pulled over. Hopping out of the car, I opened the back door in perfect time. Jonsey sprang forward, splattering chunks and chunks of vomit through her hands as snot seeped out of her nose.

"Damn, Jonsey, you a'ight?" Totta asked in a concerned timbre. "Jonzella, you okay, baby?"

"I think so," she stated before crying.

"Okay, this trip is officially cancelled. We heading back. Jonsey, you throwing up and shit, and, Jonzella, you crying. Why in the hell are you crying?" Totta inquired as I wondered the same thing.

I know it's not possible for them to know what we have done and who we are seeking, I told myself as I grabbed a rag and water bottle from the console.

"I'm just emotional that's all," she stated, wiping her face as I poured water on the rag.

"But why?" Totta probed at the same time I began cleaning Jonsey's face and hands.

Is it possible that they know their brothers snitched on us and that we must kill them? I inquired as I continued caring for the chick that I should've never been fucking with in the first place.

"I'm like this close to my period."

"Oh," Totta voiced oddly as he briefly glanced at me.

"Thank you," Jonsey voiced hoarsely as she slid back in the seat.

"You are welcome, my queen," I told her before placing the seat belt around her body.

After closing the door, I hopped in the driver's seat. Turning off the hazard lights, I jumped into the light traffic. All sorts of thoughts crossed my mind as the car was quiet. Turning onto a ramp to head back to the girls' crib, no one said a word which further raised questions in my head. Wanting to leak the press, I refrained from doing so.

Taking his seat belt off, Totta hopped his six feet two, black ass on my freshly cleaned seats, faced the ladies, and sincerely said, "Jonzella, if you don't want me, I'm cool with that. Okay? Not saying that a nigga won't be hurt because I would be, but I would let you be. If I did something to scare you, I apologize. I'll never hurt you, and I put that on my mama. I'm bold enough to tell you I love you in private...I can say that in front of Dank and Jonsey. Girl,

I love you, and a nigga ain't finna lose you. Not by any motherfucking means, you feel me?"

"Yes," she replied weakly, followed by continuing, "I just wanna go home."

"We gonna take y'all home, I promise," he replied before telling Jonsey that they need to switch places.

"Yo' black ass trippin', nigga. How in the fuck you gonna climb your tall ass all over my car?" I asked in a joking manner.

"Shut up, mane, my lady feeling sad and shit. I don't have time to be fucking with you right now. Nigga, I'll get these lil' ass seats cleaned," he voiced as he slid his tall ass in the back.

"Close yo' damn eyes when Jonsey come up here nigga," I laughed.

"Boy, if you don't hush. I'm gonna tell Geraldine on yo' ass."

"Please don't do that. I don't have time for grandma to pull out them switches nih. Snitches get stitches, remember that," I stated quickly without thinking. Soon as I said that, I noticed Jonsey shiver and look at me oddly.

"Turn the radio on," Totta voiced, changing the atmosphere.

I silently thanked him for that. The entire ride back to their crib, I was thinking heavily about their sudden mood change. I wanted to believe that they didn't know about Totta and my situation, but deep down, I knew that they knew. How was the question that I couldn't ask— just in case I was wrong about them knowing anything.

Reaching into my console for a cigarette, I was pissed that I didn't have any. God knows I had to have at least two of them. There was no telling what was going to be said once we pulled onto their street. Zooming onto the Court Street exit to visit one of their convenient stores, I saw that infamous black on black 1976 Caprice. Swiftly turning into the Chevron gas station, I placed my whip in park and asked anyone did they want anything.

"No," the ladies said.

"I'm finna get out and get my stuff, Dank."

"A'ight," I replied as I opened the door and stepped out.

"You sure you don't want anything out of the store?" Totta asked Jonzella.

Shaking her head, he simply replied, "Okay. We will be right back."

"Okay," she stated weakly.

Strolling towards the entrance door, I spoke calmly, "Woe, they acting strange as fuck. Do you think they know?"

"I was wondering the same thing. Earlier today—" he began to say until the door swung open and out stepped the infamous X.

This fine as hell, cinnamon brown shawty was the most feared woman no matter where she went. A true bad ass at the age of fourteen, she was. The biggest dope dealer in the United States, she was. No one dared to fuck with her unless they wanted their families to own a death certificate with their name on it. I couldn't lie like I didn't admire her because I did. I admired her more now since she successfully exited the game without a scratch to her sexy body.

"What it do? What it do, X?" Totta stated before dapping up the most dangerous, untouchable woman in the United States.

"What's up, Dank and Totta? I'm finally able to enjoy life. Ready to drop my load," she huffed before lightly laughing as she rubbed her swollen belly.

"I heard that," he replied as I got straight to the point.

"You got pull all over this motherfucker ... I need your help bad," I told her, staring straight into her eyes.

"I'm slowly transitioning out of the game. Therefore, you can reach out to Ruger, J-Money, or Baked. They will have all my pulls," she informed us.

"A'ight. Bet. Thanks," we stated in unison before she walked away.

"Salute," we chanted.

"Y'all gotta come out of the salute soon. Don't forget that I'm leaving this lifestyle behind, fellas. Start saluting them. Keep in mind they are ruthless savages, just like me," she yelled as she hit her key fob, which brought The Beast, what she called her car, to life. Future's song "Paradise" blasted from the speakers of The

Beast. Before we stepped inside of the store, X skrt'd off and down South Court Street she went.

Once in the store, Totta and I finished our conversation. By the time we grabbed snacks, beers, and ginger ale for our ladies, we knew what we had to do. It was going to be hard, but it had to be done. Paying the cashier for our items, we left the store— quiet as a mortuary.

Upon entering the car, I couldn't take the silence anymore; thus, me saying, "Will y'all please tell us what's really going on with y'all?"

"I'm tired," Jonsey replied quickly.

"I'm not feeling well," Jonzella stated as she lay in Totta's lap.

"Okay," I announced as I drove away.

***

It was eight o'clock at night, and the girls were still closed lipped. I was glad when Jonzella and Totta retired to her room. I wanted to talk to Jonsey— one on one.

Gently rubbing her stomach, I softly spoke, "Jonsey, I know you. What is wrong? Baby, talk to me, please," I begged as I glared into her eyes.

"Nothing's wrong with me. I'm just tired. You and I had one hell of a night/morning. I really just want some peace and quiet. Are you staying the night?" she voiced calmly as she continued to watch TV.

Caught Up In A D-Boy's Illest Love 2

"Do you want me to stay or go home?"

"Stay," she passionately said as she turned her head to me, showing her watery-filled eyes.

You know don't you, beautiful? I questioned as I continued to look at her, silently hoping that she didn't.

"Okay. Let's go shower, and then we can go to bed. How about we shower, watch a movie, and then go to sleep?"

"That'll be fine," she responded with a half-smile.

Scooping her up, I stuck my tongue in her mouth. For a minute, she hesitated; however, I wanted her tongue in my mouth. In a matter of several seconds, Jonsey reciprocated the kiss. We didn't stop kissing until we made it to the bathroom. On the way to the bathroom, we heard Totta and Jonzella chatting. I wanted to know what they were talking about, but I had bigger things to worry about. Placing my boo on her feet, I started the shower for us, followed by me undressing her then myself.

"Jonsey, you do know that I'll never hurt or let anyone harm you right?" I inquired as I pulled her shirt over her head.

"Yes," she voiced weakly, not giving me any eye contact.

"Jonsey, I need you to believe that I will never harm you. I don't know what got you so rattled, but you need to know that I'll never do anything to you. Like I said before, I really do care about you, and I mean that," I confessed after I lifted her head up so that I could look into her eyes.

"Okay," she replied as she bit down on her bottom lip.

Nodding my head, I removed the rest of her clothing, followed by taking off mine. Walking over to the short, brown rack in the bathroom, Jonsey handed me a blue washcloth as she held on loosely to a yellow one. Our shower was quiet as we bathed each other. After we washed, we dried each other off before she traced her fingers along the front of my body.

"Make love to me, please," she cooed as her hands landed on my awakening penis.

"Are you sure you want that given the state that you are in?" I inquired as I rubbed her face.

"Yes."

"Okay," I responded as I bent down to place her right nipple in my mouth.

"Mmph," she moaned lowly.

Thumbing her left nipple while sucking on her right, my dick began to press against her clit, causing her to groan my name, "Cassseyy."

"Yes, baby, yes."

Removing my mouth and hands from her breasts, I lifted her into the air and began carrying her to her room. As our tongues were engaged with one another, we heard Jonzella loudly moaning, "I do love you, Totta. I doooo."

Caught Up In A D-Boy's Illest Love 2

Safely inside of Jonsey's room, I closed and locked the door. Placing her back on the cold, white door, I lifted her further into the air so that I could have her pussy covering my face. In a flash, I was rubbing my face in between her hairless monkey. On her clit, I made slow, circular flickers, which caused her legs to shake. As Jonsey gripped the back of my head while calling my name loudly, I slid two fingers inside of her. Teasing and taunting her body, I grew eager to please her, all the while enjoying her sweet juices sliding down my throat. I took my time tasting and exploring her hot, dripping wet insides as she cooed, clawed, and lightly wept. As I ate her pussy, I carried her to the bed. Delicately putting my queen down on the cold sheets, I made love to her with my mouth and hands until she begged for me to stop.

"Casey, I can't take anymore. Please let me get on top of you," she whimpered as her legs shook uncontrollably. Before I removed my mouth from her sweet spot, I hungrily lapped her juices and talked to her.

"I'm never going to leave you ... you know that right?" I inquired as I continued to finger and mouth fuck her.

"Yesss," she whimpered from pleasure.

"Are you going to leave me?" I asked as I dipped my tongue in and out of her whole while pressing harder on her G-Spot.

"Oooouuuu...that's... my spot, Cassseeyyy!"

"I asked you a question, Jonsey. Are you going to leave me?"

"Fuckk nooo! I love this! I love us!" she yelped as she climaxed—hard.

"I love us, too," I replied as I continued raining down pleasure on her beautiful, brown body.

Eager to give her the full royal treatment, I kissed my way to her lips as my dick landed on twat. Gently placing my man inside of her, she began to cry.

"Why are you crying, my queen?" I asked as I slow stroked her body.

"I'm so confused... until I don't...I don't...know...what... to do," she whimpered as she brought her lips to mine.

"Let me ease your mind. Don't think, just feel. My lovemaking will tell you all that you need to know."

"Ooooouu... ahhhh!" she screamed as her body shook.

"Give it to me, Jonsey. I notice that you be holding that nut back. Tonight, I want it," I demanded as I began to speed up my pace.

"I don't know how," she cooed.

"Relax, baby, that's all that you have to do."

Doing as I commanded, my queen had several intense orgasms back to back to back. Her bed was soaking wet, I was soaking wet, and she was soaking wet. We slow rode each other until I couldn't hold back anymore. Our sensual noises mixed in with how we felt for each other, on top of how amazing our sex was, caused me to tell her the truth.

Caught Up In A D-Boy's Illest Love 2

"Jonsey, you are going to be my wife someday," I moaned before I spread her legs wider and let my sperm spill inside of her.

"And you shall be my husband, Casey," she stated breathlessly before I stuck my tongue in her mouth.

Chapter 3
Jonzella

Lying woke as the moonlight shined through my bedroom window, I glared into the man's face that I grew to love. Gently running my hands down his slick, wavy, coarse hair, my mind and heart were playing tug-of-war with each other. I didn't know how to break things off with us, or even if I should end our situationship. The love I had for him was like none other. The first time we met, I knew that we were meant to be. He was one beasty, stubborn nigga. Totta meant that no female could tame him; that there was no way in hell that he would submit to one woman. He let it be known that he wasn't built for a relationship, and that I shouldn't expect him to ask me to be his woman. Gladly taking on the challenge, I went in knowing that he really wanted to be tamed but didn't want to hear the backlash from the niggas in the streets.

I played the loving homie with benefits role, which I enjoyed and had amazing perks. Totta's sex game was amazing; the first time we slept together I was hooked! There was no leaving a strong, fine ass Black man who had money, wasn't stingy, and was down to earth. Truth be told, Totta and I had a lot in common, and that fact alone was the reason why I was trying to figure out how to keep him and Casey off my brothers' ass. I wanted my brothers alive and healthy as well as having a loving, joyful future with Totta.

Zit. Zit. Zit.

Underneath his pillow, Totta's cell was ringing. Not once did he stir upon the vibration from the phone. Ignoring his phone, I continued to think about how to get him and Casey off my brothers' case, if they had someone scope them out, and if Jonsey and I were a part of their game. There were so many different things going on in my head that I tuned out the vibrating phone.

Thinking of the worst that could happen to Jonsey and me, I felt that we needed a break from the guys. Our best thinking took place when they weren't in our presences. They kept us in the bed moaning and groaning about how much we care about them.

Zit. Zit. Zit.

Not ignoring the phone anymore, I slid my hand underneath his pillow and pulled the phone out. With his device in my hand, I said, "Totta, you might want to get your phone. Someone's trying to reach out to you."

With his eyes closed, Totta groggily replied, "I'm not worried about that phone. I'm where I want to be, my queen."

A smile was on my face as I began to place his phone on the bed. The moment I sat that damn thing down, it vibrated. Looking at the lightly dimmed screen, I saw a message icon that informed me

Caught Up In A D-Boy's Illest Love 2

Totta had a text from a broad named Erica. Intrigued to know why she was texting him at one o'clock in the morning, I said, "This might be a sale."

"Shid, if it is...they are shit out of luck," he replied while turning over.

Placing the phone underneath the pillow, I sighed heavily followed by sliding my body closer to Totta's. Wrapping my arm around him, he voiced lightly, "You know a nigga got mad love for you, right?"

"Yes. How many times are you going to tell me that in a given six-hour period?" I inquired curiously.

"As many times as I need to tell you. Go to sleep before I slide in between your legs again," he joked while grabbing my hand and securing it on his chest.

Smiling, I placed a kiss in the center of his back before telling him goodnight. Letting my mind relax, I felt sleep knocking at my eyelids. Halfway closing them, I felt vibration coming from Totta's phone. Moving quickly so that he wouldn't feel his phone vibrating, I snatched that annoying fucker from underneath the pillow. Someone was trying to reach out to him, and I had to know who. I had to make sure that Jonsey and I weren't in danger.

As I slipped away from my bed with his cell phone in my hand, I quietly exited my room. Standing in front of my room door, barely breathing, with Totta's phone in my hand, I unlocked his secured phone and opened the messages from Erica. When I say that woman sent him thirty messages, I meant just that. I read every one of them; all of them had me heated as fuck! I wish I hadn't looked at any of them. Not giving a damn about what he and Casey were capable of doing, I was on the path of fucking Joshua Nixon's ass up!

Opening my door with great force, I flipped on my cellphone; thus, the light coming on. With an angry facial expression, heart racing, left hand clenching and unclenching, I threw his phone at him while screaming, "Bitch, if you don't get your ass up...I know something. You finna explain to me why a bitch named Erica is texting you that she misses you, when you coming over to please her, sending you naked pictures, and why you ain't answering any of her texts!"

Stirring around in my bed, Totta turned over and said, "Mane, what you talking about Jonsey?"

"Don't play stupid with me! What the fuck is up, Totta?"

"Mane, calm down. Close the door and come lay down," he demanded as he rolled over.

Why in the world did he do that? He didn't know that he was fucking around with a certified crazy broad. I wasn't going to be playing around with his ass! Running towards the bed, followed by jumping in it, I was throwing punches on his back and head.

"What the fuck, Jonzella? You better chill out with that shit now!" he yelled as he hopped out of the bed.

Grabbing his phone, I replied nastily, "You better explain some shit to me now!"

"What you want to know, mane?" he asked while his dick began to rise.

"Who is Erica?" I inquired as I cocked my head to the right.

"A bitch I was fucking with," he answered nonchalantly.

"You still fucking her?" I asked, growling as I prayed he was going to say no.

"I cut her off last week," he replied as I felt the wind being knocked out of me.

"Wow, Totta, wow," was all that I could say as I stared at him while shaking my head.

"She means nothing to me. I only want y—" he stated before I cut him off.

"How long have you been sleeping with her?"

"Jonzella, Erica and I are no longer dealing with each other. I ended shit between the two of us. She's history. I'm focused on you and me, now."

"No, you ain't. You can't be tamed by a female, remember. Look, I think you need to go home. I'm not feeling you rig—" I began to say before I gagged, followed by putting my hand over my mouth, hopping out of the bed, and running to the bathroom.

"What's wrong with you?" he asked the moment I bent the corner and fled down the hallway to the bathroom.

Lifting up the toilet, I let the demons out. Totta was steady asking me what was wrong with me. Vomiting and shrugging my shoulders, I continued emptying my stomach. Afterwards, I lay on the cleaned toilet seat as Totta grabbed a washcloth, followed by wetting it.

"Come here, queen," he voiced as he kneeled beside me, wearing his white gym shorts.

"I need you to go home. I don't want to be around you right now," I told him as I didn't look at him.

Touching my forehead then my back, he said, "You don't have a fever, and no I'm not going home. We need to talk about Erica because I don't want to be arguing about her every time you feel like bringing up her name."

"Trust, I won't bring her name up. I keep forgetting what you said the first night we met. I'm not yours, so you don't have to worry about me flipping out like I just did," I told him as I pushed myself off the toilet.

"Don't start that shit," he commanded as he grabbed my arm at the same time I felt the need to vomit again.

Quickly aiming for the toilet, Totta said, "What in the fuck is wrong with you?"

As shrugged my shoulders, I let the demons out once again. I didn't know what the hell was going on, but I knew the shit better knock it off. I didn't like being sick, and I sure as hell wasn't pressed on missing school or work.

After fifteen minutes of being in the bathroom, my stomach finally settled, which allowed me to brush my teeth without gagging. On my way to my room, I felt like shit. Slowly getting into my messed-up bed, Totta stepped into my room and said, "Jonzella, I only want you."

"Totta, go home. We'll talk eventually. Right now isn't the time. Okay?"

"No," he responded as he closed my bedroom door.

"Look, Totta...we ain't a good match for each other. Let's just cut shit short between us. It was great between us, and I don't regret one moment," I stated, trying not to break down in front of him.

"I'm not going anywhere, other than the store to get you a ginger ale, orange juice, and some crackers. So, lie down and rest," he voiced in a caring tone as he strolled towards me.

Knowing why he wouldn't leave me alone, I stared at him while shaking my head, all the while wanting to burst his bubble. Not knowing what he would do if I did say something about my brothers, I knew that it was in Jonsey's and my best interest to keep my mouth shut—tight.

"Stop being stubborn," he stated before planting a kiss on my forehead, followed by rubbing my stomach.

Not able to help asking, but I had to know, I voiced lowly, "Did you sleep with her unprotected? Did you sex her like you do me?"

When he wasn't too quick to say no to both questions, I knew the answer was yes. Smirking as tears slid down my face, I yelled loudly, "Get the fuck out of my house, and don't bring your black ass around me no more! Don't call or text my motherfucking phone! Don't even speak to me in public! I'm so done with you!"

Growing angry with me, he snapped back with, "You knew what the fuck you were getting into when you signed on the dotted lines of sliding down this dick of mine. I don't trust no female. I struggle daily with giving my all to you, and you only, in hopes that you will tame me like I want you too. A nigga fucked up, Jonzella."

Crying and laughing at his dumb comment, all I could say was, "Oh, you don't trust no female, huh? Oh okay...please get the fuck on. This conversation is over with. Have a great life, Mr. Nixon!"

"Mane, I didn't mean it like that!"

"Whatever," I shot back, rolling my eyes.

For the next fifteen minutes, we went back and forth; it was paused when I pushed him out of the way. My hand was covered over my mouth as I ran down the hallway to relieve my throat of the trapped bile. As I passed Jonsey's room, I was surprised that neither she nor Casey showed their faces.

Standing behind me as I dry heaved, Totta said, "You might be pregnant, Jonzella."

With an attitude, I nastily shot back with, "Like hell I am. Nigga, I been sliding them Plan B pills down my throat. This is a side effect of taking the pill. I don't have time to be no one's baby mama...especially, yo' ass! Now, get the fuck out of my house."

I knew he was beyond pissed the moment he said, "Let me get the fuck out of here before I tear your head off!"

Ignoring his comment, I cleaned my mouth followed by cleaning the toilet. Stepping out of the bathroom, I heard him mumbling to himself and shuffling shit around. *Finally, he getting the fuck away from me,* I thought as I ambled towards my room. Soon as I got into my comfortable place, that motherfucking nigga was making up the bed. Coming to a complete stop, I glared at him with my hands on my hip.

Placing his eyes on me, he sternly voiced, "I'm not finna argue with you. When I come back from the store, I'm gonna lay beside and hold you like I've been doing since we been fucking around. So, get yo' sick ass in this damn bed, Jonzella, and rest all your nerves. Shit."

Not in the mood to argue with him, I politely got my ass in the bed; however, I was pouting like hell. I wanted Totta's ass out of my presence, and the only way I knew to do that was to lock the front door as soon as he waltzed out of it! I didn't want a dick that belonged to everyone in the city; the same dick that probably was trying to kill my brothers! Nawl, he had to go; simply put.

Chapter 4
Totta

Out of all the times I left my phone around Jonzella, she has never gone through a nigga's shit. She barely looked at the damn thing, so I didn't know what had her so antsy to check into my device. She was truly on some more shit; I hope it wasn't the shit that Dank and I suspected they were on—like them knowing that we were looking for their brothers, or the simple fact that their brothers were the reason detectives were looking at us.

Strolling inside of the hood store, I kept to myself as I saw Erica and Bianca at the cashier register. Placing her eyes on me, she sucked her tongue while sighing.

"Guh, ain't that Totta?" her cousin, Bianca, inquired loudly as I picked up a gallon of orange juice.

"Yep," Erica voiced just as loud as Bianca.

"So, what the hell going on between the two of you? Wasn't he just at your crib Thursday?" she asked nosily as I grabbed a pack of saltine crackers and a large ginger ale.

"Yep," she replied as I strolled towards the register.

Erica's items were bagged. An idiot would wonder why she was still hanging around the empty store; yet, I wasn't no idiot. I knew that she was hanging around for me, and I wasn't going to pay her any attention. She was part of the reason my queen was at the crib feeling some type of way.

"So, you ain't gon' say nothing to me? Did you get my messages? Why are you acting like this, Totta? I didn't have any problems out of you Thursday... so, who really got you pissed off? Is it that little bitch in my Calculus II class?" she inquired as she toyed with her fingernails.

Ring. Ring. Ring.

Ignoring the old fuck toy in front of me, I pulled my cell phone out of my pocket. Upon seeing Dank's name, I quickly answered the phone.

"Yo," I replied as I put my items on the wet counter.

"You good, mane?" he inquired as I heard a door close behind him.

"Yeah, I'm good...shit, I think," I told him truthfully as Erica kept running her mouth.

"Dude, where the fuck you at?" he questioned in a confused manner.

"The hood store. You want something up outta here?"

"Nawl. You got some 'Rillos already?"

"Nawl. I'm finna cop some though."

"I know damn well you hear me talking to you, Totta. How you gone tell me not to be fucking with no other nigga than you, yet you treating me like this?" Erica stated angrily as she pushed me.

"Ah...my man, let me get six regular Swisher Sweet added to my tab. A large meat lover's pizza with extra cheese, and a large ham and turkey salad," I voiced as Dank was talking about the shit Erica was spitting in the background.

The Arab dude rung up my items, gave me the total, followed by telling me it would be twenty minutes before the pizza was ready. Handing him the money, Dank was telling me that Jonzella was crying her ass off, which I kind of figured that.

"Mane, she came and locked the door when you left," he laughed and then continued, "She meant she didn't want your ass coming back."

Grabbing my things, Erica was still standing close by with her arms folded and pouting as I replied to Dank's comment, "She could've locked me out. I went and got a key made to the front and back door. Jonzella better stop playing with me. I'm already fuming about her taking them damn Plan B pills."

"You worried about a bitch that ain't glad to get pregnant and start a family with you. Meanwhile, you ditching the one woman that's truly dedicated to starting a family with you...you really are stupid, Totta," Erica yelped as she ran behind me.

"Hold on, Dank," I told my partner as I evilly glared at Erica, which made her come to a complete stop.

"Bitch, if you don't sit yo' money hungry ass down somewhere. Starting a damn family should be the last thing on your agenda.

How about understanding that simple as arithmetic first. Don't come for no woman that is above your worth net!" My ear was ringing after I focused back on my call with Dank.

"Dude, really?" my partner laughed.

"The bitch can't even add, subtract, multiply, or divide that well; yet, she wanna get in a class that Jonzella's in...just to be damn messy," I huffed as I hopped in the front seat of my whip.

"You surely know how to pick them, don't it?" he laughed.

Becoming annoyed with him on my line, I replied "Shut the fuck up," before hanging the phone up in his face. Out the corner of my eye, I saw Erica jumping into a red, new model Camry. Seeing the car back away, I slouched down in the front seat of my car.

While waiting on my pizza to bake to perfection, my thoughts ran to the one woman that had me all over the place. A nigga didn't know how to function properly without talking, texting, or seeing Jonzella. The thought of losing her was driving me crazy. I know for a fact I would be going on a killing spree if she decided to stop fucking with me for real. Who she was as a person helped me understand myself better. I loved being a street nigga, and I had to admit that I admired being a lovey-dovey type of dude, too. Jonzella was the only woman that could pull that side out of me.

Ring. Ring. Ring.

Looking down at my phone, I saw Erica's name displaying across the screen. Ignoring her call, I quickly placed her on the block list.

Normally, I wouldn't do that, but given the circumstances, I didn't need any more issues with Jonzella's ass. Glancing at the clock on my phone, I gladly stepped out of my car. Running inside to retrieve my pizza, I informed the Arab man on what I wanted on my salad.

Within three minutes, I was starting the engine on my whip. Peeling away, I zoomed back to Olivia Drive with a mission of how I was going to get back in the good graces of my queen. Parking besides Dank's whip, I shut off the engine, followed by grabbing the food and drinks. Opening the door, Dank was talking mad shit.

"You hung up the phone like a little bitch. Ole sensitive ass broad."

"Shut yo' ass up. Don't be joking too much. You know karma is a bad, thick broad. She will have you doing the same shit."

Handing him the pizza, I closed and locked my whip. Strolling towards the front door, I caught a glimpse of Jonzella running to the bathroom with her hand over her mouth.

"Plan B pills my ass," I huffed as I shook my head.

"You think she preggo, woe?" Dank asked curiously as we ambled through the front door.

"Do shit stink?"

"Yep." He laughed, causing me to slightly laugh before saying, "Then, that's your answer."

As he closed the door behind him, I walked into the kitchen and flipped on the light. Seconds later, Jonsey and Dank strolled into the kitchen.

"Sorry, we disturbed y'all," I told them as she opened the fridge.

"Y'all okay," she replied lowly as Dank grabbed plastic plates.

Pouring orange juice into a small glass, I grabbed a pack of crackers. Before I left the kitchen, I asked them, "How many times Jonzella threw up?"

Staying in the clear, Jonsey didn't answer my question, but my homie did. "Two."

"Thanks, man," I told him before skipping towards the back of the ladies' crib.

"Jonzella," I called out as I passed Jonsey's room.

"Wh...wha—" she began to say before dry heaving.

Knowing her location, I pulled up at the bathroom as if it was fifteen minutes to closing time at McDonald's. Seeing her bent down over the toilet, I started with my shit.

"So, the Plan B pills make you do all of that? How many did you take? When did you take them? When is your period supposed to come on, or is it late? Shid, I ain't heard you complaining about your stomach since the beginning of December, Jonzella."

Removing herself from the toilet, Jonzella ignored me as she tried to get her breathing under control. Turning on the cold water, she grabbed her toothbrush and toothpaste, followed by applying the minty teeth treat to the blue and green bristles on her toothbrush.

"Umm, are you going to answer me or what?" I inquired, impatiently.

Brushing her teeth, she shook her head.

"Why not?"

That heifer shrugged her shoulders, followed by sticking up her middle finger. Placing the crackers and juice on the hallway floor, I waltzed into the bathroom and stood behind Jonzella. Rubbing on her stomach, she tried to push me away.

"Did Zaddy Totta put a baby in there?" I asked hopefully as I pressed my hardening dick against her butt.

As she pushed me back, I laughed. I knew that once she was done rinsing her mouth, Jonzella was going to curse me out. Handing her a dry wash cloth, I watched her lightly dap her face as I continued to drill her with questions about her period and that Plan B.

Growing annoyed with me, Jonzella yelped, "Can you please go sit the fuck down somewhere, or better yet, go lay down some fucking where? All these damn questions...a bitch ain't up for it, Joshua Nixon! You working my last one and half nerve."

In the hallway, Jonsey was laughing as Dank said, "Damn...the *last* one and half nerve."

Caught Up In A D-Boy's Illest Love 2

Opening the door, poor little Jonsey had tears running down her face as she continued to laugh. Flipping off Dank as Jonzella flew past me, I told Jonsey and my homie, "Y'all get on my nerves. Go make a baby or something."

"Errr," Dank voiced loudly, caused me to laugh as Jonsey quickly ceased her laughter to say, "Oh, no, I have things to do."

The serious, yet scared, look on her face made me become even more of an asshole, "You better watch your man then. I think he might try to trap you."

"Jonzella!" Dank yelled loudly. "Please come get your petty ass nigga."

Strolling towards Jonzella's room, I loudly sang, "Birds of a feather flock together. Jonzella ain't gonna be the only one with a swollen stomach."

"Get yo' in the doghouse ass in here, Joshua Nixon!" my queen yelled in an agitated tone.

Closing the door behind me, Jonzella was giving me the evil eye. Stripping out of my clothing, I slowly walked towards her. With a smirk on her face, she stated, "Don't be rattling my sister's nerves like that. She will burst out crying in a minute. I don't have time to be dealing with her, on top of dealing with not feeling well."

"Okay," I replied as I watched her nibble on a cracker.

Lightly pushing her further into the bed, I stared at the beauty that captivated my mind. My hormones raged as I was trying to not be considerate of her physical state.

"Totta," Jonzella softly said.

"What's up, my queen?"

"I know what you do for a living, and who you are," she voiced, not looking at me.

Instantly, my dick went down. At the mentioning of who I am caused my heart to drop in my ass, my mouth became dry, and I was at a loss of how to form a single word. While looking into her face, all I knew to do was tell the truth. Placing my hand on top of hers, I opened my mouth to try and defend Dank's and my case against her brothers, but Jonzella continued speaking.

"Totta, you are a male whore. I knew that the moment you opened your mouth to me. You are also a hustler; I knew that the moment you paid for your items and mine, not to mention the types of niggas that flock to you. You are a killer. How I know? That shit comes with the territory of being a dope boy. I say that to say this. I don't care how you treat me. Just please don't hurt my brothers, sister, or parents, hurt me instead. Punish me for what my brothers are bringing against you and Casey," she stated in a shaky tone as tears slid down her face.

I thought I wanted to tell her the truth, but the thought of having that AIS number for the rest of my life, cut that shit short. Playing dumb was the best thing that I could do.

"What are you talking about?"

"Don't insult my intelligence, Totta. I'm being serious."

"I'm not. A nigga just don't know what you are talking about."

Sighing heavily, Jonzella glared into my eyes. The look she gave me made a brother sink further into her soft mattress. While feeling some of her emotions, I felt the blues coming on. Seeing that she had something to tell me, I rubbed her thigh followed by saying, "Talk to me, queen."

Crying, she replied, "I don't want any blood shed on anyone's end. I love you, I do. But, they are my family. They took me in when my men addicted mother left me stranded for days at home without food, water, electricity, and love. I can't have anything happen to them as I can't have anything happen to you."

"Can you please stop talking about shit that I don't have any clue about, Jonzella Brown?" I questioned in an annoyed timbre while clenching my jaws.

"Totta?" she called out lowly as she lay in my arms.

"Yeah," I replied in a tone that I hoped she understood. A tone that meant kill the conversation.

"Where did you go some weeks ago?" she inquired curiously at the same time I became suspicious of her questions.

Hopping out of the bed, I scrambled to put my clothing on. Not answering her, I knew my homie and I had to get the fuck away from the ladies. I loved little mama true enough, but not enough to have a fucking AIS number.

"Where are you going?" she asked while crying.

"Shid, you wanted me gone so a nigga finna get the fuck up outta here."

"Totta, whatever you are thinking, please don't. I'm not that type of person," she pleaded while sobbing, lightly.

"Shid, I can't tell. I'mma holla at cha," I told her as I aimed for her bedroom door.

Soon as I placed my hand on the doorknob, some type of object flew at my head. Without seeing what she threw at me, I ran towards her. As Jonzella tried getting out of the bed, I quickly snatched her up by her hair.

"Nope, you bold enough to throw something at me, you better be bold enough to hear what the fuck I'm saying to you, Jonzella," I growled at her while I shoved her onto her back, putting my hand on her neck—applying no pressure.

"The damn thing wasn't going to kill you," she lowly sobbed.

"The next time you throw something at me, Jonzella, I'm going to tear up the place. You got me?" I growled.

"I hate you! I should've left your black, no-good ass right there on the candy aisle ogling me!" she screamed while fighting to get away from me.

Moving away from her, I resumed walking to the door. On the ground was the object that she threw at me— a motherfucking pregnancy test with two, strong pink lines! Seeing that I had gotten her pregnant didn't put me in a better mood, it only pissed me off more. Knowing that I was angry for her mentioning her brother and highly believing that she was on some setup type of shit, I should've walked away without saying a word.

Yet, my idiotic ass spat, "It was nice knowing you."

Chapter 5
Jonsey

What I thought was going to be a fun and relaxing weekend getaway with the fellas and my sister turned into a scary, yet pleasure filled, weekend. The last episode between Jonzella and Totta took a toll on me and Casey, causing him to leave right along with Totta. We barely talked as much as we used to. A part of me wondered was that for the best given the circumstances surrounding my brothers. Feeling two-sided about the situation, I decided to lay underneath Jonzella as she tried to come to terms with everything that happened with her and Totta.

My poor sister cried all day yesterday. I felt so bad for her. In between crying, she weakly said, "Jonsey, he told me nice knowing you after he saw the pregnancy test. That's some hurtful shit."

Not wanting to have any ill feelings towards Totta, I tried to stay on the outskirts of things as Casey suggested that I should; however, after what he told Jonzella, I didn't think I could even speak to him, right now.

Ring. Ring. Ring.

Grabbing my phone off the back of the sofa, I exhaled heavily; my poor little body was exhausted from the sexing that Casey and I had been involved in all week. Seeing his name on the display screen, I quickly answered the phone with a smile on my face.

"Hello," I spoke sweetly while staring at the front door, hoping he was going to say to open it.

"What you doing?" his deep, sexy voice inquired.

"Lying on the sofa watching TV. What you doing?"

"Chilling at my grandmother's house."

"Ahh. You coming by?"

"Not tonight."

"Awww, me missing you," I cooed, not trying to coo or let him know that I was missing him. *What in the hell is wrong with you, Jonsey? Your brothers told y'all parents that Totta and Casey were the last ones that saw the two dudes alive,* I thought as he chuckled before saying, "You'll see me soon."

"How soon, though?" I voiced, letting him know that I was disappointed.

"Not sure yet."

"Okay."

"I don't hear Jonzella. Where she at?"

"Finally went to sleep."

"What do you mean *finally* went to sleep?"

"She's been crying, followed by throwing up or dry heaving ever since y'all left the other night."

"Damn, tell her I said I hope she feels better soon."

"I will."

"Well, let me get off this phone. I just called to check on you."

Feeling disappointed that he was getting off the phone with me so quick, I replied sadly, "Okie dokie."

Hanging up the phone, immediately I knew that things were going to be different for all of us. I was going to see less of Casey as Totta was going to dismiss himself out of Jonzella's life. Feeling sorry for my sister and self, I flicked off the TV and ambled towards my sunshine filled room.

Closing my bedroom door, I retrieved my finance book. I didn't need to overly concentrate on anything in particular; I needed an outlet from what I was feeling. Thirty minutes into my studies, my mother called my phone.

"Hello," I chimed.

"Hi, sweetheart. How are you?" she voiced sadly, causing alarm to rise in me.

"I'm okay, and you?" I asked with a shaky tone.

"A mess, honey, a pure fucking mess," she stated before breaking down.

I tried my best to calm my mother down, but it didn't work. She ended up making me cry. I was so thankful when my father got on the phone.

"Hi, Daddy. What's going on? Are Kenny and Kevin alright?" I asked, trying to stop sobbing.

"No, baby, they aren't alright. The doctors said that they are unresponsive, and they have declared them as being brain dead," he stated strongly as I heard my mother in the background howling.

"My poor, poor babies. I want the largest amount of money placed for a reward to anyone that know details about who shot my sons!"

Crying as I understood what my father said, I replied with shaky lips, "We are on the way."

"There is no rush. You girls file the proper paperwork with your school to go on bereavement for a couple of days. Finish this week of school, and then you guys will return back home Sunday morning in preparation for school on Monday. Understood?" my dad announced sternly.

"Yes, sir. We love you."

"We love y'all the most," he replied before telling me that he would talk with me later on.

Soon as I hung up the phone, Kyvin was calling. On the second ring, I answered his call.

"Hearing the tone in your voice, I'll take it as you've talked to Mom and Dad," he responded in a sad tone.

"Just hung up the phone from with Dad," I cried as I thought about my two pain in the ass brothers that I would never get a chance to talk shit about.

"When are you and Jonzella going up there?"

"Friday."

"Why not sooner?" he asked in an agitated tone; one that I was not up for.

"Because Dad doesn't want Jonzella and I to miss too much of school. He wants us to file the proper paperwork that would not interfere with our attendance," I told him with as much attitude as I could.

"Umph...well I will check on y'all throughout the week," he quickly spoke.

The thought of Kyvin feeling some kind of way about my statement made me say, "Look, I don't know what the fuck is your problem, Ky, but I am the last one to piss off. Matter of fact, don't worry about calling and checking in on me and Jonzella. We are motherfucking fine!"

Ending the call, I placed my oldest brother on the block list. He was already skating on thin ice from our Christmas conversation. If he knew what was best for him, he would find him something safe to do!

Throwing my finance book on the floor, I broke down as I cried for my parents, brothers, and Jonzella. Tired of crying, I grew angry; I was pissed at my brothers for always staying in some shit. I was beyond pissed at the thought that Totta and Casey may have sent someone to cause harm to them. I wanted some answers from Casey, and I be damned if he wasn't going to give them to me.

Hopping to my feet, I quickly dressed in a pair of black pants, black sweater, and black Nike boots. Snatching my purple jacket from the coat hanger on the back of my door, I slipped my cell phone in the side pocket before fleeing down the hallway. After scribbling a note on a piece of paper for Jonzella, I threw it on the sofa at the same time I retrieved my keys.

Walking out of the door, a light breeze ran across my face—causing me to shiver. Zipping up my jacket, I took a look around the small knit community of Olivia Drive. There were four brown and white duplexes in front of Jonzella's and my duplex, which was blue and white. On our side, there were three duplexes. My and Jonzella's living quarters were in the middle of the much need renovation duplexes. The grass was green and well-manicured. The trees in the yards were fully blossomed and healthy.

Walking towards my car, I noticed that many of our neighbors didn't have any visitors. Everyone that lived on my street was either college students or older couples with no children. It was a perfect street to live on. No crimes, no police doing checkpoints, and certainly no ignorant people blasting music. Unlocking my car door, I noticed a black SUV with tinted windows slowly creeping up the street. Panicking, quickly unlocked my door, followed by hopping inside. Once inside, I locked my doors and started the engine. Not wasting anytime with pulling away from my apartment, I zoomed down the narrow, curved road. Coming to a complete stop, I pulled my phone so that I could call Casey.

With shaky hands, I slammed the phone into the passenger's seat followed by skrting away from Olivia Drive. As I topped the slight hill, I looked to the left and saw Casey and Totta's truck parked on the side of a yellow and brown single-family home— Casey's grandmother's crib. Zooming up McQueen Street, I was overwhelmed with the blue emotion. Seeing that the traffic was clear for me to make a left turn on Ann Street, I took off as if someone was behind me.

My only destination was changed due to the fact that I didn't have the balls to confront Casey with what I learned. Not the type to put myself in danger, I let my mind get off that subject. Approaching the turning lane to jump on the interstate, I did so. As I drove up the steep ramp, the only place I knew that I wanted to be was a park; at least, I could run and cry without anyone staring me in my face.

In six minutes, I was pulling into the park. It was filled with children and adults of all sizes, shapes, and color. The large-sized park had the prettiest green grass one would ever see; today, there several groups of people playing football and soccer. Three different play areas for children of all ages, a tennis area, and the perfect incline and decline running area, which surrounded the entire park.

Parking my vehicle at the end of the parking lot, I took off my seat belt and relaxed. Completing several inhales followed by exhaling, my mind traveled to my brothers, and I burst into tears. I cried until my voice was hoarse, until my chest was hurting, and until I was simply just plain damn tired from crying.

Shutting off the engine, I put my keys and cell phone in my pocket, followed by getting out of my car. While locking my doors, I realized the best way to relieve my mind of the torment and frustration within was to run the large track. I took five minutes to stretch my body appropriately before jogging; the last thing I wanted to do was have muscles cramps or to tear a ligament. Afterwards, I started out jogging. Halfway through the track, I sprinted and ran towards the end. By the time I got to my starting point, I was full blown running, shedding tears, and praying for my family. Lord knows that Jonzella and I needed him the most right now, especially knowing the men who could be responsible for their current state.

Chapter 6
Dank

While Jonsey was running and wiping her face, I pondered what had her so upset in the car that she cried for fifteen minutes straight and was still crying as she ran through the paved walkway in Vaughn Park. Seeing her in that state did a mental on me; I desperately wanted to get out and be there for her, but after the conversation Totta and I had yesterday morning, I thought it was best to chill out with Jonsey for a little while.

"Totta, pull off," I instructed as I had the urge to hop out of his uncle's truck.

"A'ight," he replied as he put the gearshift in drive.

"No Love" by Future played, causing Totta to turn it up. In seconds, the woofers in the back came to life. With a blunt in my right hand and a cup filled with Henn in the left, I had to start the song over from the beginning. Turning the radio up louder, I began to sing along.

"I'm missing all yo' touchin', I ain't fell in love with no pussy," I rapped along as Totta chimed in while jigging along to the beat.

Skrting out of the park, zipping through a quiet residential community, we fucked up the conservative side of town. Since our mothers got us whips, the blasting of music, speeding, and driving while under the influence was our thing. Close to the end of the song, that fool had to replay the song again. This time I was hanging out the window— doing the absolute most; I was ready for Montgomery Police Department (MPD) to pull up on us. I would gladly pay any amount of ticket that we got. I was in my feelings about the shit that was going to take place between Jonsey and me, and this was the only way I knew to calm down— well, other than bodying a nigga or three.

Ring. Ring. Ring.

Turning down the radio as I pulled my cellphone out, I saw J-Money's name displaying across the screen. Answering the phone on the third ring, I piped in the phone, "Talk to me."

"You good? I see ya hanging out the window and shit," he chuckled.

"Yeah, I'm good."

"A'ight. I was just checking on you my nigga. Shid, we shooting ball on the Nawfside at the community center ... y'all balling?"

"Shid, I ain't balling ... y'all niggas messed up my hip. I'm cooling, but Totta might ball wit' cha," I told him as Totta replied, "A nigga ain't balling today. Catch me next week, and I'll be out there whooping on they heads."

"Mane, tell that nigga to put his money where his mouth is. I got two stacks on the game," J-Money voiced in a hyper manner.

Relaying the message to Totta, all my partner could say was, "Bet that shit up, my nigga."

After J-Money confirmed the time, date, and location of where the betted basketball game was going down, we ended the call. As I sank back in the passenger's seat, I was in desperate need of slanging my piece in a bitch's guts. Roaming through my phone, I stopped upon seeing Jonsey's name. Knowing well what I wanted to do and how I wanted to do it, Jonsey's wasn't the best candidate. Quickly scrolling past her name, I came upon Trasheeda's name. Wasting no time on pressing the call button, I licked my lips as I got ready to hit her with my favorite line.

"Hello," she answered the phone seductively.

"What you doing, woman?"

"Shit, cooking. What's up?"

"I wanna slide through and hang out with you for a little while. A nigga miss you, girl," I voiced as Totta snickered.

"Boy, bye. I don't have time to be the last-minute female. I told you I don't have time for your games. How about this? I'll call you when or if I want some of you," she stated before hanging the phone up.

"Woe, did she hang the phone up on you?" Totta asked before busting out laughing.

"Hell, fuck yes...now, watch in five minutes, her trifling ass gon' call me back...wanting a nigga to pull up," I informed him with a smirk on my face.

Under five minutes, my cell phone rung, and I'll be damned if it wasn't Trasheeda.

Answering the phone, I said, "Yeah."

"Nigga, bring your black, eleven gold having ass over here. And you better not stand me up like you did last time," she huffed.

With a smile on my face, I said, "Unlock the door. I'm two minutes away from your crib."

"I told you...I know my part-time team players." I laughed at the same time Totta shook his head and said, "You wild, kid. Aye, I need you to do me a favor before you get yo' dick wet."

"What up?"

"I need you to call Jonsey and check up on Jonzella for me," he replied quietly as he slowly mashed down on the brakes.

"Like I asked you earlier today when you sent me on that mission... why can't you call her?"

"I'm ashamed of doing so. Mane, I was beyond confused, frustrated, and pissed off at the early morning Saturday events. I did and said some shit that I didn't have any business doing or saying. Just make this one call for me, please," he begged.

Wanting to know what he said and did that had him ashamed to call Jonzella, I asked, "Totta, what the fuck did you do and say?"

Once again, he retold me the story of him and Jonzella talking about him punishing her instead of her brothers. In the wee hours of the morning when we left the females' house, that foolish nigga didn't tell me that Jonzella threw a positive pregnancy test at his head, followed by him telling her some off the wall shit.

All I could do was shake my head at him before saying, "You fucked around and got the chick pregnant...on the low, you actually was hoping she was. Then you turn around and say some shit like that, after she comes to you with the don't hurt my brothers skit...she told you she was willing to suffer for what they were trying to do to us. Mane, shawty got some ill love for you, bro, and it has nothing to do with the fact that you got her pregnant. Are you really going to be dumb all of your life, Totta?"

Not saying a thing to me as he made a left turn into the nigga nicknamed neighborhood called The Four Way, I stared at my partner and couldn't utter a damn word. Before I tempted to dive deep in some cat, I had to know what he was thinking.

"When she presented the shit about her brothers to you, did you almost choke her out?" I inquired as he pulled into Trasheeda's yard.

"Nope," he replied, looking at me.

"Did you want to tell her the truth?"

"Yep."

"Why didn't you?"

"I didn't want either of us to have an AIS number; the less she knows the better. I played dumb until she asked about the business trip we took earlier this month. I hopped my black ass out of that bed. I felt as if she had a wire on or some shit."

Trying to place myself in his shoes, I knew I would've done the same thing; however, I wouldn't have told her that it was nice knowing her after learning that I got her pregnant. Women don't forget how you treat them when they inform you that you have knocked their asses up. Broads become vicious as fuck if you don't handle the situation the right way—their way!

"Mane, call her yourself. That's your job, not mine. Come back and scoop me up in three hours," I commanded as I extended my balled-up fist to him.

After dapping me up, I hopped out of the truck and proceeded towards Trasheeda's front door. Ringing her doorbell, I opened the golden screen door followed by opening the tan, wooden door. Soon as I stepped foot in her front room, the chick had red rose petals scattered across the clean, tan carpet while several candles were lit atop the entertainment center. 90's R&B music was playing at a nice decibel as she seductively sashayed in a tight green shirt that had the word slay written in gold.

"Damn, you trying to make love to the kid, ain't it?" I chuckled as I locked the screen and front door.

"Nawl," she laughed, showing her platinum bottom grill before continuing, "I'm gon' make you appreciate me. The same chick you be ditching for those unappreciative little girls you be fucking with."

Thirty minutes of kicking the bo-bo with Trasheeda, we got down to some dirty business. Ensuring that she didn't put her hands on my condoms, I kept them close to me. She wasn't going to get me if I just happened to close my eyes while she rode me to hell and back to Earth.

***

After Totta picked me up from Trasheeda's crib, my mind was back on Jonsey. For the life of me, I couldn't understand why my feelings didn't do what I needed them to do. I didn't have time to fall in love with her; she could cost me my life.

"What are you thinking about?" Totta questioned.

"About Jonsey," I told him as I fired up a blunt.

"Oh," he quickly said while looking at me.

"Do you think they will talk to their parents about us?"

"I don't know. I hope not. I surely don't want to—" he started to say before cutting himself off. There was no need in me telling him to finish his sentence because I already knew what he was going to say.

To stop his mind from wanting to act on killing the females, I brought up him calling Jonzella to check on her.

"Nawl. I'm not doing that. I'll know how she's doing through you. You are going to ask Jonsey for me," he spat as I handed him the blunt.

"Like I told you earlier, I'm not going to do it. That's your job. Why won't you check on her, woe?"

Sighing heavily, my partner for years replied seriously, "I don't want to hear her voice in case I have to kill her while she's pregnant with my seed."

With nothing to say, I just stared at him. There was so much that I was supposed to say behind his comment, but my mouth wouldn't corporate. Deep down, I knew that there was a possibility that we had to knock the females off. We didn't know exactly what they knew; however, for Jonzella to tell Totta not to hurt her brothers, the females knew something.

"What do you suppose that we do?" Totta asked, interrupting my thoughts.

"I say that we tail the girls for some days. Check out their mental, and we can go from there. Whatever you do, don't say shit to Danzo. His ass will have them killed without a moment's hesitation," I voiced while placing my feet on top of my coffee table.

Confirming that he agreed with my statement, Totta nodded his head while tugging on the tightly rolled blunt. Grabbing the remote for the radio, I was in the mood to hear some trap music, and not the new age bullshit. My mind was set on Young Jeezy. With *Let's Get It: Thug Motivation 101* cd already locked and loaded, I turned up the volume as the beat dropped to the first song "Thug Motivation 101".

Passing the blunt towards me, Totta hopped up, jigging to the song as he rapped along. Lying back on the sofa, I was bobbing my head along while saying, "Ayyee." As I began to enjoy my high, my thoughts of our meth selling business came to mind. Realizing that we been more focused on finding the snitches, we were getting low on the ice. Turning the volume down on the radio, I called out to Totta.

"What's up?"

"We low on work. Since, we used to cop dope from Baymatch. What do you think about copping strictly from J-Money?"

"Shid, it wasn't like we weren't getting the work from him anyways. Why fuck with anyone else when we've been supplying the city thanks to The Savage Clique."

Nodding my head, I was glad that he didn't see an issue with working directly with J-Money.

"We need to hit him up, and let him know how much we need," I informed Totta as the second song "Standing Ovation" ended.

"Bet. How much are we placing an order in for?"

"Income tax season is in...the meth order needs to be tripled," I voiced as I dapped the roach of a blunt in the ashtray.

"You don't want to fuck with that boy?" he inquired, referencing on heroin.

"Nawl, my clientele don't fuck with that shit. Do yours?"

"Only about twenty of them. They pay money out of the ass for that shit. Last week, one of my junkies and his wife were whooped badly behind them not leaving the superb, five bedrooms, three-bathroom home they owned."

"Explain that shit, my nigga."

"The junky told the heroin dealer that he needed to credit a large quantity of that boy. Immediately, the dealer wasn't hearing that noise. That's a lot of money to be paid. So, the junky put up his crib and the furniture inside if he didn't come through with the money."

"Well, damn!" I said, shaking my head.

"So, your flunky is on meth and heroin?"

"Yep."

"Those are expensive ass drugs. What he do for a living?"

"A top-notch lawyer and his wife is a surgeon."

Shaking my head at the foolishness of people with the brains to make a difference in the world, I had to know was the wife on some shit too. "Is she on that shit, too?"

"Who knows," Totta huffed while strolling into the kitchen.

Caught Up In A D-Boy's Illest Love 2

Knowing that he was going to raid my refrigerator, I yelped, "You gon' start putting some groceries in this motherfucker. Shit, you eat more than me, and I live here."

"Shut yo' whining ass up."

"And make sure you clean up your mess too, nigga. You know I hate when you leave shit out of place and crumbs all over my counters and tables."

"Once again, shut yo' OCD having ass up," he laughed as he savagely rambled through my cabinets.

Three minutes later, Totta was plopping his rusty ass in my recliner with a fat Italian sandwich and a plate filled with chips and four pickles. With a smirk on my face while shaking my head, I picked up my cell phone.

"I'm finna rap with J-Money. You want me to put in a small order of heroin for you?"

"Shit, yes," a stuffed mouthed Totta stated.

"A'ight."

Pressing the send button besides J-Money's name, I stretched out on the sofa. In no time, he answered the phone. After the pleasantries were said, I gave him a coded order for our dope. In a coded response, he told me how much, when it would be ready, and the location to pick it up from.

Once the call ended, I looked at Totta and said, "Tomorrow at two p.m. We'll meet him at the community center to pick up the work."

"A'ight."

"Finish up that sandwich. If we keeping an eye on the females, then we need to stroll through their street," I commanded as I hopped off the sofa.

"Shit, I can eat and ride. You driving Unc's truck?"

"Yeah."

"Cool," I responded as we headed to the front door.

From the time I closed and locked my front door, we were quiet as a church mouse. If I was in the lane called confusion, I knew my homie was too. He had a bigger battle to deal with, given how he truly felt about Jonzella and her pregnancy. I, on the other hand, had to figure out was my freedom more important than dissing and hurting Jonsey— a sweet, caring, and loving individual.

While I was in deep thought about the one woman whose smile would make my heart do the A-Town stump, I was pulling onto their street. As I slowly drove up the road, Totta was sitting up in the seat—scoping things out.

"Shit, are they even there?" he asked aggressively.

"I saw a lighting coming from Jonzella's room," I told him as I turned around in the dead-end curve.

"Turn the lights off and pull on the curb," Totta mumbled.

With a worried look on my face, I said, "What you finna do?"

"Finna make sure everything is mine."

Busting into laughter at that fool, I had to crack on his idiotic ass.

"Dude, how in the fuck can you say some shit like that when you told Jonzella it was nice knowing you?"

"Mane, look, don't ask me no questions," he voiced in an upset tone as I heartedly laughed at the nut.

Stepping out of the truck, Totta flipped me the bird. Increasing my tickled state, I whipped out my phone to text Jonsey.

Me: What you doing?

Some time passed before I saw Totta walking from the right side of the house. Soon as he hopped in the car, he asked, "Did you text Jonsey?"

"Yeah. Why?"

"I overheard her telling Jonzella that you texted what you doing," he replied. Knowing that he had more to say, I kept quiet.

"Yo' ass been gone for a minute...you must was eavesdropping on them?"

"Yep. Jonzella's window was slightly open."

"Okay, so spill the beans," I told him, urgently.

"Pull off. We don't have to keep a trail on them," he smiled happily.

Cutting on the lights, I pulled away from the curb. As I slowly drove down the road, I said, "Explain."

"Let's just say that those females got the illest love for us, and I need to make things right between me and Jonzella," he voiced while grabbing his cellphone out of his pocket.

Caught Up In A D-Boy's Illest Love 2

With my heart and mind at ease, I was relieved to know that we didn't have to hurt them in the worse way!

Chapter 7
Jonzella

Tuesday, January 17th

I woke up extra early so that I could visit Cope, a pregnancy resource center, before going to school. At eight o'clock a.m., I was dragging my exhausted, sick body inside of the homely environment. Ten minutes of filling out a piece of paper, talking to a nice, sweet, white woman, followed by peeing on a pregnancy test, I was beyond ready to find out how far along I was; I had to sort things out.

"Ms. Brown, according to the last time you had a period, you are five weeks and four days," she voiced sweetly as she filled out a piece of paper.

Not knowing what to do with the paper, I asked, "What am I to do with that paper?"

"You will take this paper to your doctor's office. If you are going to apply for Medicaid, you will take this paper along with an application to the Human Resource Department on Mobile Highway," she voiced soothingly.

"Okay. Thank you," I replied sincerely.

"You are absolutely welcome, sweetheart," she stated as she motioned for me to walk with her.

Caught Up In A D-Boy's Illest Love 2

As I strolled out of the medium-sized, baby-proofed room, she continued talking, "We have excellent parenting classes. We give you mommy bucks to purchase anything out of our mommy store. Items range from car seats, cribs, bassinets, pampers, clothing, bottles, and things of that nature."

Wanting to know more about the parenting classes, I asked. For fifteen minutes, she gave me a tour of the area where parenting classes took place. Knowing that I would need to take those classes, I told her that I wanted to sign up immediately. After I received helpful parenting information, on top of registering for the classes, I fled to my car. The smell of McDonald's was doing a number on my stomach.

Starting up the engine, my phone began to ring. Seeing that it was Totta calling, I sent him to voicemail. Not thinking twice about not talking to him, I zoomed towards ASU. With the radio on low, I zoned out as I drove the short distance to my school. I was glad that I only had two classes: one at nine and the other at eleven. My cozy bed was calling me.

Ring. Ring. Ring.

Taking my eyes off the road for a split second, I saw Jonsey's name, and I immediately answered the phone.

"Hello."

"Hey. Where are you?" she asked as I heard a door closing.

"I'm pulling up at school."

"Why you left so early? You could've told me that you were gone. I was screaming your name like I lost my mind," she fussed at me, which I found to be cute.

Smiling, I said, "Sorry. I didn't want to wake you. I had to visit Cope before I came to school. The way my body is setup, I won't be worth a quarter after my second class."

"Ohh. What did they say?" she inquired as I heard air which I knew was heat blasting through her phone's speaker.

"I'm five weeks and four days pregnant."

Sounding sad, she asked, "Are you okay?"

Chuckling at my sister's overly emotional tail, I replied honestly, "Yes. I'm okay, minus the sickness. Totta doesn't want to be a part, and I'm okay with that. I made my bed, and unlike my birth mother, I'm going to be the best momma I know how to be. I will show my child the exact love your parents showed me."

"You better or I'mma kick your ass," she joked.

"And you better," I laughed as my line beeped. Taking the phone off my ear, I saw Totta's name. With a smirk on my face, I sent his ass to voicemail.

"Jonsey, I'm going to head into my class early. I will see you once our classes are over with. K?"

"K. Love you," she sang.

"Me love you more," I voiced before hanging up the phone.

Caught Up In A D-Boy's Illest Love 2

Parking my car as close as I could to the building that housed both of my classes, I hopped out with my bookbag as a group of females had their eyes on me. Locking my door, I strolled towards the broads. When I say those bitches didn't take their eyes off me, I meant that.

It got to the point I had to ask, "Umm, is there a booger on my face? Is my hair a mess?"

"Nope," they giggled, which made me slow down in front of them.

"So, what's up, ladies?" I inquired as my phone began to ring. Annoyed with the possibility of Totta blowing up my phone, I sighed heavily.

"Nothing," three of them replied as one lone monkey stood still while glaring at me with her mouth stuck out.

"Okay. Y'all have a great day," I replied sarcastically before taking my eyes off them.

Walking away, one of them hoes mumbled something followed by the rest of the girls giggling. For the life of me, I couldn't understand why females like them existed in the first place. Topping the hill where my first class was located, I noticed the bitches were walking behind me. As I saw those crows, I also saw Totta's black ass creeping up the road.

"Fuck!" I yelled as I knew he saw me. How? The bastard pressed on the gas pedal.

Not in the mood to argue with him at my educational institution, I was on the verge of running until I realized that I didn't need to be face down, ass up in the toilet.

The best thing I could do was pretend like I didn't see his ass while I crossed the street— in front of his speeding car. Blasting the horn as if he was a mad man, I ignored him as I kept on walking. Slamming on the brakes, Totta rolled down that damn window and said, "Jonzella, don't make me nut up in this bitch early in the morning!"

Now who in the hell tells someone some of that nature when they were the reason things went sour between them? My ignorant ass baby daddy, that's who! Jumping to his level, I politely said, "And don't you make me act up in this bitch early in the morning. I'm not up for your shit, they shit, the devil's shit, or the shit that's going to come out of my ass after lunch. Now have a great fucking day, Joshua Nixon!"

Walking off on his ass, I thought he got the hint. Obviously not! That fool swung me around, which made my stomach do numbers, and I was beyond pissed that I had to cover my mouth from keeping vomit spilling all over him.

"Shit, queen, I'm sorry. Forgot that you got the queasy stomach," he voiced sweetly as I released the demons in front of a large oak tree.

Afterwards, I rinsed my mouth with the travel-sized mouthwash followed by brushing my teeth— right underneath the tree. Quickly getting myself together, I glared at the fine specimen in front of me before bucking my eyes and asking him what he wanted.

"You sending me to voicemail. Why?" he asked as if he really didn't have a single clue.

Giggling, I saw the ghetto runts a few inches away from us, I said, "I don't have time for you, that's why. I got bigger things on my plate than you. So, like you told me, it's nice knowing you."

Strolling away from him, Totta grabbed my book bag, while saying, "Jonzella, I'm sorry. I got pissed…like really, really pissed. I shouldn't have told you that. I was wrong. Please forgive me."

Nodding my head, I replied casually, "I forgive you. Now, goodbye. It was truly nice knowing you. Thank you for the blessing you have bestowed upon me."

"You think you just gon' walk out of my life…with my seed, Jonzella?" he growled.

"Shid, you already did that. So, what the fuck you talking 'bout, dude?" I asked with an attitude, realizing that if I didn't leave his ass standing there I would be late for class.

"Don't piss me off, Jonzella Brown!" he yelped as he flinched his jaws.

"I have no reason to piss you off. I'm just done with you, the thoughts of us having a future, and all that shit. You destroyed that the moment you learned that I was pregnant...in which, I thought you would've been excited about. Anywho, I got a class to attend. Don't you have some bitches waiting on you?" I voiced nastily before taking off.

"You ain't gon' stop fucking with me. I'on give no fucks about that shit you talking about! I'm that crazy, ignant nigga that got you pregnant. You and my seed belong with me!" he yelled as I slid into the building.

Letting Totta's ass slip from my memory, I focused on the task that Professor Lewis assigned us last week. The hour and thirty minute class went by in a hurry, which I was very thankful for. Heading out of the front door, one of the broads from earlier bumped into me.

"Umm, excuse you," the multi-colored weave wearing, dusty foot broad stated with an attitude.

Lord, you know that I'm trying to do right. Why are you sending the devil towards my way? I thought as I voiced loudly, "Bitch, you bumped into me. So, what the fuck? Do you have a problem with me or som'?"

"I sure the fuck do!" she yelped, causing students to come to a halt as they placed their eyes on me.

"Shit, then I gots a problem with you. What's up, bitch, square up," I replied sternly as I dropped my book bag at the same time Jonsey pulled my arm.

"No, ma'am. You can't be cutting up like this, Jonzella. It's not just you anymore," Jonsey voiced calmly as the dusty worm kept talking her shit.

"You right, Jonsey...you are absolutely right," I replied as I eyed the bitch who had beef with me.

Putting my backpack on my back, I began to stroll away until the whore said, "That's why I'm fucking Totta, and have been for quite some time. Ask him who Erica is. How you like that, bitch?"

My insides turned upside down, the muscles in my legs seemed as if they wanted to crumble underneath me, and my throat went dry at the same time the tears acted like they wanted to form in my eyes.

Turning around slowly, putting up a fake happy façade, I clapped my hands a while before saying, "Oh, you the bitch that's finna supply our child with all types of stolen shit. Girl, I will hand him a list of shit so he doesn't have to spend his money. Ericaaa, oh yeah, you the backup bitch he calls when I was having periods, or when I didn't want to give him none. Damn...oh, yeah, you the type of bitch that can most definitely have him now. I cut his ass loose, just in case your ears were filled with earwax, earlier today when he pulled down on my ass, trying to make a scene since I won't talk to him. Baby girl, please, get my baby daddy off my ass!"

"Gladly," she replied as I turned my back to her.

Not wanting to let anyone see me sweat, I burst out laughing. Only Jonsey knew that I was angry and ready to bust that nigga's head.

"Are you okay?" Jonsey asked as we strolled towards the administration building.

"Yep. I'm ditching my last class. Are you in?" I asked her through clenched teeth.

"Yes, ma'am. I gotta make sure you stay your ass out of trouble."

Fifteen minutes in the administration building, I was about to lose my mind. I was ready to get ahold of Totta and tell him some lovely things. I was glad when Jonsey and I informed the head people that we had a family emergency. They acknowledged that we weren't going to be in class for the duration of the week. Walking as fast as I could to my vehicle, I told Jonsey to go home.

"Like hell I am. I'm going where you are going," she yelled.

"Okay. Well, suit and boot up, bitch," I laughed as I unlocked my car door.

After starting my engine, I fled out of the school's parking lot. Aiming for Totta's apartment in The Four Way, I was violating all types of traffic violations. Ask me did I give a fuck; nope, I surely didn't! In eight minutes, I swerved my whip beside his. Shutting off the engine, I hopped out the car as if I was set on fire!

While I was running towards his apartment, Jonsey was yelling, "Don't you cut up!"

Ignoring her, I ran up the flight of stairs. With his door key in my hand, I was eager to get that fucker opened. Upon reaching his door, I unlocked it. The look on him and Casey's face as I stormed in slamming his 60' inch Sony flat screen TV on the ground, kicking the X-box and motherfucking games on the floor would've had the next person laughing.

"Oooh shit," Casey voiced as he picked up his feet.

"You better calm your pregnant ass down," he said before I cut him off.

"Bitch nigga, if you say one more motherfucking word, I will set this bitch on fire!" I yelled as he stood to his feet while Casey was glued to the sofa.

"All I'm saying is, you can't be cutting up like that with my baby in your stomach," he voiced softly.

"Nigga, it ain't even a baby yet. The thing like a small pimple or some shit. You say another word, Totta, and I promise you I will set this damn place on fire!" I told him as ran to his kitchen.

By the time Jonsey came running in, I was on a warpath. After I opened every cabinet door, I was cursing his ass out while slanging dishes across the room, aiming for his head, or throwing them against the floor and walls.

"Shit, Jonzella, you almost hit me," Jonsey whined.

"Well, you better duck and dodge these motherfuckers. I told yo' ass to stay in the car anyways," I voiced as I wasn't done showing my ass in his kitchen.

Going into the last opened cabinet, I grabbed every one of the plastic cups and paper plates, turned on the stove, and set them bitches on fire all the while saying, "You won't have a fucking dish in this bitch to eat on, cook with, or drink out of. You don' fucked with the wrong hormonal broad. Yo' ugly black ass!"

"Jonzella, you can't be cutting up!" Jonsey yelled, turning on my heels, I lifted up my shirt, showing my chrome .22, I spat nastily, "Shid, watch me!"

Opening the refrigerator, I snatched all the damn racks out. Food, pots, pans, and beverages spilled as Totta sighed heavily, "Where is the sensible woman I've been fucking with?"

"Bitch, she gone!" I yelped quickly as Casey said, "Shid, Totta, I'mma get on up outta here! I feel that my life is in danger."

"Mane, don't you leave me in here with her. I don't know who that person is," he replied oddly as I maneuvered to his bedroom.

"Jonzella! Please, honey, let's go. You messed up his home enough," Jonsey voiced sweetly as I tore up Totta's room.

Caught Up In A D-Boy's Illest Love 2

After I went crazy in his bedroom, I moved my ass to the bathroom. I was waiting on him to say something smart or try to calm me down. I was going to beat his ass with the shower rod. Smashing the mirror with his toothbrush holder, I laughed sinisterly before yelling, "You wanna fuck these 'build-a-bitch from my homegirl's closet' type of hoes. Oh okay."

Turning the knobs on the tub and sink faucets on full blast, I grabbed the cleaning products by the twos, opened them, and started slinging them all over his bathroom. Wanting to start a fire, I thought against that; doing that would possibly involve the police, and I wasn't about that life!

Strolling out of his bathroom, into the front room, the stares they gave me told me that they were shocked and partially frightened. As I was about to give him a grand speech, my cell phone rang. Pulling it out of my pockets, my biological mother's name displayed. Her calling fueled the fire.

"And what in the whole fuck do you want this morning, Renee?" I voiced nastily.

"I wanted to talk with you, baby. Mommy, really needs you," she cooed.

"I'm quite sure I'm the last person you need, Renee. Where all those dicks at that you left me for, huh? Call one of them motherfuckers, and tell them that you need them," I replied spitefully before hanging the phone up in her face.

"Oh, my godddd," Casey voiced as he covered his mouth; any other time I would've laughed at his stupid ass, but I was not in a laughing mood.

"Jonzella, you tore up my home...queen, talk to me," Totta voiced calmly as I felt his eyes on me.

In a split second, I went from angry to sad.

"Jonzella, I think it's time to go home," Jonsey cooed as she ambled to me.

"You are right...it is time to go home. I'm so done with this sorry ass, this low-paying state, and the nasty, fuck anything type of pussy ass nigga I've been dealing with," I sneered as I briefly placed my eyes on Totta before walking towards the door.

"Ain't gon' be too many of your pussy ass or bitch niggas," Totta voiced sternly.

Turning around on my heels, I damn near pushed Jonsey out of the way. Glaring into his eyes as I placed my hand on my .22, I growled, "You are whatever the fuck I call you! If you don't like what I call you or how I see you, then stay the fuck away from me. How 'bout dat? Go call that thirsty ass whore Erica. I'm sure she's waiting on that call since I told her that I'm done wit' yo' ass! *And* that I'm glad to hand her over to you."

"Jonsey, can you explain to me what in the hell Jonzella talking about?" Totta voiced.

"Don't explain shit to him. He's done too much to our family anyways. Fuck him! Let's go!" I commanded, walking away from his filthy ass home.

As we traveled halfway down the stairs, I heard Totta say, "I'm going to strangle that bitch Erica for getting my queen upset. Dank, I swear if Jonzella loses my seed, I'mma murder Erica and her entire fucking family!"

Chapter 8
Jonsey

Friday, January 20th
Myrtle Beach, SC

Since leaving Totta's house on Tuesday, I had a total of twenty-five voicemails from Casey and thirty text messages from him. After reading his messages and listening to his voicemail, I couldn't lie that I wasn't smiling and feeling warm inside; however, I remembered what I said about not dealing with him anymore. As bad as I wanted to confide in him, I knew that it wasn't the best thing to do since Jonzella and I were about to stroll inside of Grand Strand Medical Center to say our final goodbyes to Kevin and Kenny.

"Are you ready to do this?" Jonzella and I asked each other in unison.

"Not really," I replied honestly.

"Well, we don't have no choice. We been in this parking lot for thirty minutes. Let's spend time with their bodies before we never see them again," she said before blowing her nose.

"Okay," I replied as I thought of how perfect the day would've been for cuddling underneath my covers while snacking on golden Oreo cookies.

Caught Up In A D-Boy's Illest Love 2

The sky was gray with a speck of sun rays trying to come through. The wind was extremely breezy, which I hated. After observing the beauty of the calm sky, I opened the door. Soon as my body caught a whiff of that winter air, I wanted to close it back. Ready to say my final goodbyes to my siblings, I found enough courage to get my tail inside of the hospital within seconds of closing the door.

As we entered the quiet, well-decorated establishment, we caught a glimpse of Kyvin on the phone. Looking directly at me, that fucker turned his nose up and turned around. He was on some ish, and I was the right one to give it to him today!

"Did you see what that idiot just did?" I asked Jonzella.

"Yep, and don't you get out of character. This is not the time, nor the place," she replied calmly while clearing her throat several times in between her words.

Knowing what that meant, I asked sincerely, "You nauseous?"

"Yes, all these smells are doing a number on me. We can't stay long. I'm not ready to tell Mom and Dad about the pregnancy."

"I'm glad you said that, because I was thinking that I don't want to stay no longer than twenty minutes. The plan is for us to fake as if we are tired," I told her as we were close to Kyvin.

"Gotcha," she quickly replied.

Our oldest brother was chatting away on the phone in a low timbre. Hoping that I would behave, I patiently waited five minutes for him to end his call; when he didn't, I copped an attitude.

I know damn well you see us here. That damn phone call ain't that important, nigga," I voiced sharply.

Turning around to look at me with an evil eye, Kyvin said into the phone, "I will call you back soon as I can."

"I guess one of those thugs got you out of your shell," he hissed as he waltzed up to Jonzella and gave her a hug.

"And I guess your bootyhole licking friend got you feeling yourself, to the point, you are becoming a total asshole."

"Okay, you two, please stop. I don't know what in the hell is going on with y'all, but it needs to stop. Mom and Dad need us right now, and all this extra bickering can cease," Jonzella voiced sternly, looking amongst Kyvin and me.

Nodding his head, Kyvin said, "You are right, Jonzella. Let's get up here and do what we came here to do."

"Are they in separate rooms?" Jonzella asked Kyvin as we waited for a few people to exit the elevator.

"No. You know Mom wasn't having that," he lightly chuckled as we stepped inside of the cold, musty smelling elevator, trying to lighten the mood amongst us.

"No, she wo—" she tried to reply before gagging.

Laughing, Kyvin said, "You still got a weak stomach?"

Caught Up In A D-Boy's Illest Love 2

Nodding her head, I was relieved when the elevator door opened. The last thing Jonzella needed was to puke everywhere. Silence overcame us as we followed Kyvin to the room our brothers laid.

Upon entering the room, instantly Jonzella began to cry as my eyes watered while thinking, *I will forever hate you, Totta and Casey.* Our father strolled towards Jonzella. Still weeping, she placed her hands over her mouth as she walked into our father's arm.

My mother began praying, which caused me to walk over to her. Gently rubbing her back as I said, "I'm so sorry, Mommy."

After she finished praying over my brothers' souls, she looked at me with carefree eyes and said, "They are in a better place now. God and I had a long talk last night."

Nodding my head as my heart ached, I lowered my body to hers. With open arms, I grabbed my mother— giving her the biggest heartfelt hug. As we held on to each other, Jonzella's sobs were light as she walked to Kenny's side. Rubbing his face with a weak smile, she said, "Now, who am I going to tease? I'm really going to miss you, brother. I love you. Watch over and protect us all."

Ending the comforting, warm embrace with my mother, I stood erect as I watched Jonzella plant a kiss on Kenny's forehead. Leaving his side, she maneuvered to Kevin's bed. She glared at his body. Shaking her head as the tears streamed down her brown, glowing face, she announced lovingly and in a joking matter,

"Don't you get up in Heaven doing the most. I fa da hate for God to put you in time out because you trying to throw a party in His palace."

Upon her remark, everyone laughed. No matter where that fool was at, he always had to cut up in a good way. Not one time had Kevin been the type to cry or feel the blues. He was the type of person to turn a funeral into a party while the preacher is performing a sad, powerful going home celebration.

The room became quiet as Jonzella's cell phone rang. Pulling it out of her pocket, she silenced it and slammed it roughly back into its rightful place, all the while mumbling something. From the look on her face, I knew who it was.

Breaking the silence amongst us, my father said, "So, how was the drive up here?"

"Quiet," I told him truthfully while giving him my full attention.

"How's school going?" my mother asked while sitting back in the chair with her legs folded.

"Good," I replied as Jonzella said, "Okay."

"Y'all have two more semesters to go. What are y'all plans afterwards?" our father asked at the same time Kyvin sighed.

"Hopefully, I'm going for my bachelor's degree in Physical Therapy," Jonzella said. I could've kicked her ass for saying hopefully; she was going to start an entire lecture about that one damn word!

"What do you mean by hopefully, Jonzella?" Father asked curiously while planting his medium-sized brown, rounded eyes on my sister.

"Just...just...anything is liable to happen, and I hope to have the strength to march forward on my bachelor's degree," she commented in a shaky timbre.

"I know your grades are spectacular because I call and check on them. So, what life's obstacle could get in the way of you achieving your goal?" he inquired as if he was Sherlock Holmes.

On the verge of opening her mouth, Kyvin beat her too it. "Pregnancy could derail her, Father."

With a thousand daggers that I shot to him, Kyvin looked at me with a nasty facial expression.

You stupid son of a bitch, I thought while eyeing him.

"I know Jonzella wouldn't think of doing anything that would take her off the course of her dream, Kyvin. Now, would you, Jonzella?" our father voiced sternly while Kyvin sighed nastily.

"No, sir," Jonzella replied with a straight face.

What the fuck is wrong with Kyvin? Why he acting like a pure asshole today?

"Good," our parents voiced in unison.

The room fell silent briefly before Kyvin started chuckling. With all eyes on him, he finally decided to show his ass.

"Why do y'all hold these girls up on a freaking pedestal? They are no different than Kenny, Kevin, and me. Since, we were younger...everything has always been about them. Why don't they have a leash on their necks as we did?"

Shaking my head while looking at Jonzella, I stood to my feet. As I was about to walk off, father told me to have a seat. Doing as I was commanded, he said, "We didn't and still don't have to worry about the girls doing things out of the norm, Kyvin. Your mother and I had a tight leash on you fellas, and look how y'all turned out."

Kyvin's face turned from cinnamon brown to black in a matter of seconds before saying, "Not one time have I broken the law. Not one time have you caught me stealing money from either of you. Not one time have I disobeyed anything y'all have instructed. So, do *not* put me in a category with Kenny and Kevin. I finished school at the top of my class, graduated college in the top five of my class, and I'm doing damn great as a starting out lawyer."

My father stood to address Kyvin; however, my mother was the one that spoke up.

"Yes, you have done all those great things, Kyvin. No, we haven't had any trouble out of you. We would take Kenny and Kevin's criminal ways over a son that prefers men any day. That lifestyle is not right, son, and you know it."

"Oh, milord," Jonzella voiced lightly as she perched her ass on Kevin's bed, looking amongst Kyvin and our parents.

With angry eyes at our parents, Kyvin shot back, "I guess it's cool to lay up with thugs, drug dealers, and do God knows what with those kinds of men, huh?"

"It's not the same as sleeping with the same sex," our sassy mouthed mother piped back, standing to her feet.

"Let me tell your ass something, Kyvin, you keep on playing with me and what I want from you, and I will do something to you that you never thought that a mother could do. Don't you *fuck* with me. Your father and I have been patient as long as we can be. We are not accepting of that lifestyle, and never will be."

Before storming out of the room, he looked at each of us. Shaking his head, he stated, "This is the last time you will hear or see me. You can't tell me how to live my life...just as I couldn't tell Father how to live his."

"And what does that mean?" Father asked in a strong commanding timbre.

Sighing heavily with a sneaky smile on his face, Kyvin announced loudly, "I couldn't stop you from screwing one of the business partners at my job. I couldn't tell you that it was wrong to commit a sin against God and your marriage. I couldn't stop you from sleeping with Jonzella's mother, now could I?"

With a loud gasp from Jonzella, myself, and mother, my father voiced loudly, "Get the fuck out of here with those absurd comments."

"Absurd you say? Okay, Mom, did Father tell you that he was coming to North Charleston on a business call two weeks ago? Last year, when we visited Quebec, Canada, wasn't Father missing for almost seven hours? When we first welcomed Jonzella to the family, didn't you recall seeing him and Jonzella's mother having sex in the backyard? I want you to say no to all of those questions, Mother," he laughed sinisterly before continuing, "I was right by your side every time. Especially, when he was digging in and out of Renee without a condom on."

"Get the fuck out of here!" my mother yelped as her body shook uncontrollably as tears flowed down her beautiful, hazelnut face.

"Gladly," Kyvin voiced as he turned on his heels.

Soon as the door closed behind him, my mother burst out in tears. Afraid to comfort her, my father strolled towards the window and began looking out of it. Jonzella looked at me before mouthing that she was ready to go. Trying to figure out the best words for us to escape, our father relieved us.

"I think you girls need to go to our home and rest. We will see y'all for dinner," he stated with his back turned to us.

"Yes, sir," we replied in unison as our mother continued to weep.

Before leaving, Jonzella and I hugged our parents, followed by giving our brothers a farewell kiss on their foreheads. Stepping into the hallway, Jonzella and I didn't say a word. As I looked at her, I noticed that she was avoiding placing her eyes on me.

"I don't know how true Kyvin's comments are, but I don't want you to feel any kind of way. Okay?" I told her as I connected our hands together.

Staring at the ground, she sadly said, "I do feel some type of way because I knew what was going on between Renee and Daddy."

Chapter 9
Totta

"Yo," I called out to Dank as he was munching on his lunch.

"Yeah," he said as he wiped the sides of his mouth.

"Have you talked to Jonsey, yet?"

"Nope."

"She ain't texted or nuthin'?"

"Nope."

"You texted her?"

"Shit, my nigga, you know I did. What's up with all these damn questions, woe?" he inquired as he looked at me with bucked eyes.

"Mane, look, I'm tired of Jonzella sending me to voicemail. I just wanted to know have you talked to Jonsey," I replied in a frustrated manner before sighing sharply.

"So, what are we going to do?" he asked curiously.

"Shid, create me a Facebook page," I responded seriously.

Spitting chewed sandwich out of his mouth from laughing at me, I hollered, "Nigga, get that shit up! You know my stomach weak upon seeing shit like that."

Not able to speak right away, Dank cleaned up the mess which was on my dashboard and on his pants leg. Shaking my head, I said, "I'm serious. I'm finna sit my ass right here before going in Momma's crib. Jonzella going to talk to me one way or the other."

After his laughter ceased, he spoke, "You desperate if you are creating a Facebook page."

"Extremely," I said as I began the process.

As I handled my business, Dank put his phone in his face. Ignoring him, I was setting up my page. By the time I halfway completed the setup, I said fuck the shit. Going to the search bar, I typed in Jonzella's Facebook name. Soon as her profile popped up, I was one thirsty ass nigga while I hit the message button.

Sending her a lengthy message, I was fuming that she hadn't reached out to me. Halfway through with what I had to say to her, my baby sister, Joniece, tapped on the window while hollering, "Momma, said get yo' pussy hungry ass in the house!"

"Got damn it, now!" Dank spat before bursting out in laughter.

Ignoring my sister and my homeboy, I finished my message to my queen. Soon as I was done, we hopped out of my whip. Dank was talking shit as I heard Momma yelling, "I'm finna cuss Totta's ass out. I told him 'bout coming up in here fucking with my damn cookies!"

Instantly, Dank was kneeled over in laughter. When he got the chance to speak, the silly fool said, "I'm finna post up and laugh my ass off. Momma Shirl finna get in yo' ass."

"Shut the fuck up. I didn't know she would get off this early," I replied casually as I became a punk. Only my momma could make me soft and bow down as if I was a young boy.

Before I got the chance to open the screen door, she bust the screen door open while angrily glaring at me with her hands on her hips. In three seconds, I knew Shirley Nixon was ready to tear into my ass. She had on her work uniform, which were scrubs and a pair of New Balances. Her neck-length, auburn hued hair was pulled into a neat bun.

Taking a quick look at Dank, she said, "Dank, did you help his ass eat my cookies?"

"No, ma'am," he quickly replied.

"Was you with him when he ate my cookies?" she inquired as she pulled the three switches, which were braided together, from behind her back.

"No, ma'am," he replied as he moved away from me while trying to suppress his laughter.

"Okay, baby, well get yo' black ass in the house before I put the switches on you, too."

"Yes, ma'am," Dank replied before he started to walk forward. Soon as he was near my momma, he pressed his arms and legs together as he quickly slipped into the house.

"Come on and get these over with, Totta. I don't feel like chasing you. Come on with it," she piped, walking forward as I walked backwards.

"Momma, come on now. I'm too old for this. I was going to buy you the cookies. You got off too early. I wasn't expecting you home until four-thirty," I said, trying to reason with her.

On the porch, momma's cheerleaders, my two sisters and Dank, came out, screaming, "Get him! Get him!"

As she laughed at the fools on the porch, she took off running towards me. Not the one to stand for no ass whooping from my momma, I took off running. I was a certified criminal; I was known from outrunning the police. So, I knew if I got out of her yard, she wasn't going to catch me. Gunning out of her yard, I was gone. There was no way in hell she was going to hit me with those thick ass switches. The last time I stood like a G for eating up her cookies, she broke the skin off my ass!

Halfway down her street, I heard a couple of the homies yelling before laughing, "Boy, you must've ate them damn cookies, again. Miss Shirl gon' get yo' ass."

Not looking back, I said, "Shit ye—"

My sentence was cut short as well as my running. Those damn switches connected against my back. One would've thought I was a slave the way I yelped, "Ouuuch! Shit, oh, milord! When you learned to run that fast, Momma?"

Swinging and maneuvering every way I did, Momma said while laughing, "I told yo' ass the next time you ate my cookies, I was gone tear off in that ass. You know I don't play about my Pepperidge Farm cookies, Totta."

The street was on fire from laughter and jokes. Parents my mother's age was laughing while rooting, "Get him, Shirl!"

Folks had their phones out. I was pretty sure that I was going to be on Facebook within the next two minutes. I tried every damn thing to shake my momma. Her ass was on me like shit on flies. Those licks were wearing a nigga down, so I stood in place and took four licks. The fourth lick hurt like hell. Before I knew it, I took off running. This time I left her ass in the middle of the street, laughing. Soon as I was near her house, I saw Dank had tears streaming down his face. Not wanting to stop in case she wanted to hit me some more, I threw him the keys and said, "Nigga, pick my ass up on the next street!"

Three houses away from my momma's, I heard her yell, "Boy, stop running. I'm done."

"No, ma'am. I'll come back when I get you them cookies!"

In full pursuit of the street I needed to be on, I was one hurting guy. My ass, dick, back, neck, arms, and legs were on fire. I had to know where in the hell did she get all that energy from to hawk me down like that.

Soon as I arrived on the next street, Mr. Franks, the neighborhood oldest pervert, was sitting on his porch.

Chuckling, he said, "Damn, them cookies must be mighty tasty if I see you running like that every two weeks."

"Mr. Franks, them cookies ain't worth it no mo'," I replied seriously as I saw my truck pulling in front of Mr. Frank's home.

"Damn, Shirl, got you good this time, huh?" he continued at the same time Dank hopped out of the driver's seat laughing, hard!

Ignoring the old fart, I said, "Mane, get back in the driver's seat. Momma, don' whooped on a nigga good. I ain't messing with them damn cookies no mo'."

Slowly getting my hurting body in the passenger's seat, Dank asked while laughing, "Yo' house?"

"Hell nawl! Wal-Mart, nigga. I gotta bring a truce between me and that woman. I'm don' eating up her cookies. She whooped a nigga all on his dick and shit," I said in a hurtful tone as Dank burst out laughing.

Pissed off at him laughing at me, I turned the volume up on the radio. 2 Chainz "I'm A Dog" blasted through the speakers, causing me to bob my head. Rapping the words, I sat back as comfortably as I could. Pulling into Wal-Mart's parking lot, my cell phone began to ring. With my cellphone in my hand, I saw my lawyer's name displaying. Quickly turning down the volume, I told Dank, "Lawyer, calling."

Sliding my hand across the answer option, I said, "Hello."

"Mr. Nixon, this is Attorney Price. How are you today?"

"Good and you?" I voiced as casually as Dank parked my truck on row five.

"Great, thanks for asking. I have some wonderful news for you," he voiced happily.

Sitting up in the front seat, I said, "Spill it."

"The charges against you fellas have been dropped."

With a smile on my face, I had to know why— even though, I had a pretty good idea as to why.

"How? What changed the prosecution team's minds?"

"The witnesses' parents pulled the plug on them an hour ago," my lawyer said in one breath.

"Well, damn. What happened to the guys?" I inquired nosily as if I didn't know.

"They were shot, several times."

"Wow," I replied quickly before continuing, "The prosecutors aren't going to try to mess with us over that, are they?"

"Nope. Out of state, and it has nothing to do with the state of Alabama. Truth be told, they were hesitant on using their testimonies anyway, since they weren't trustworthy."

"Okay."

"Well, have a great day," he voiced.

"You as well."

Ending the call, I was about to inform Dank of what Attorney Price had to say until his phone started ringing.

"Our lawyer?" I inquired.

"Yep."

"Great news," I sang before he answered the phone.

The call between our lawyer and Dank took the same amount of time. While they were conversing, I hit up Danzo, even though Attorney Price was going to call him. Dank asked the same questions I did. I was very sure that Danzo's nutty ass was going to ask them as well. The reason I decided not to tell our lawyer that Dank and I were together was just in case he was on some fluke shit. Regardless how much money we paid that white man, Dank, nor I, trusted him.

Soon as he hung up the phone, Dank looked at me and said, "At least we know where the girls at."

Nodding my head, I said, "Yeah, but I'm hoping mine comes back home."

"She will," Dank replied before saying, "give me your money. I'm ready to get the hell out of this store."

Handing him the money, I told him what type of cookies to get and how many bags. Soon as he hopped out of the driver's seat, followed by rounding the front of the vehicle, I saw Erica speaking to Dank.

Smacking my mouth, I nastily stated, "That bitch better not come over here with that extra shit."

I be damned if Erica didn't stroll her behind to my whip. Quickly locking the doors, I sat back with my phone in my hand. I had tinted windows, so she didn't know if I was in my whip or not. However, she knew someone was inside because Dank's ignorant ass left it on. As Erica tapped on the passenger's side window, I ignored her. Seeing Jonzella's profile picture pop up on my screen, I eagerly opened the message. As I tried to read my girl's message in peace, that was until Erica said, "I know your black ass in there, Totta. So, let the window down and be a man. Face me, nigga."

Tuning her out, I continued to read the messages as Jonzella sent them off. By the time a brother got to the last part of her first message, I saw three separate, long paragraphs and three dots after the last paragraph. Before I knew it, I yelled, "Now, got damn, Jonzella, you ain't giving me enough time to respond to the first one! Shit!"

"Nigga, that girl ain't stun' you. Why are you running behind her when you can have a woman that'll be dedicated to you?" Erica replied with an attitude.

Placing my eyes on the first word in the second paragraph, I was frustrated! That damn woman sent me three more paragraphs. Saying to hell with all that reading, I pressed the telephone option. As I was putting the phone to my ear, Erica said, "That bitch ain't coming back! So, why run behind her."

That sentence was the reason why I rolled down the window and spit in the bitch's face, followed by saying, "Get yo' dusty ass on. A nigga don't want you!"

As Erica gasped and wiped the loogie, Jonzella said, "What, Totta?"

While explaining myself to Jonzella, Erica was banging on the window while talking mad noise.

"See, Totta, I don't have time for this shit. You begging me, yet, you around that bitch, Erica. I tell you what make nice with her. Make sure you get the hoe—" she said before the line went dead.

With anger soaring through me, I tried calling her back only to see the words Facebook User.

"What the fuck!" I shouted as I realized my queen blocked me.

With a nut basket screaming and banging on my window, I grabbed my pistol from the console and hopped out the truck. Snatching the bitch towards me, I pressed the gun to her head and said, "Bitch, the next time you approach me...I will blow that dry ass scalp from underneath that stanking ass weave cap!"

Looking at me with a scared facial expression, Erica tried to say something, but nothing came out of her mouth. Her eyes were darting towards the individuals who had stopped to look at what was taking place. In my current state, I didn't give a damn about them looking. All I cared about was informing Erica how serious I was about her not being near me.

Glaring into her eyes, a stench hit my nose so heavy until it was unbelievable. Immediately, I knew what it was. Growing angry with the cunt, I spat, "Did you just piss?"

"Yes, I'm scared as hell right now. Totta, I've never seen you like this," Erica voiced as a tear slid down her face.

"Good. Now, go away pissy pussy," I replied while laughing as I eased the gun away from her head.

Running away from me, those that were looking went on about their business. Plopping down in the front seat, Dank was dragging his ass while walking behind the truck. Soon as he hopped in the front seat, I questioned loudly, "What in the fuck took you so long? I don' got harassed, had to draw down on Erica, and I got blocked from Jonzella's page."

Laughing, he replied, "Damn, you had one hellava day, my nigga. Let me get yo' grumpy ass home, immediately!"

Not seeing a damn thing funny, I replied in an annoyed tone, "Fuck taking me home right now. I need to deliver them cookies to momma."

As he burst out in laughter, I angrily spat, "Mane, once you drop them cookies off. Drop yourself off at yo' damn whip. I'm tired of dealing with you. All that giggling and shit running my blood pressure up."

"Nigga, shut the hell up and create another Facebook page. Stalk that lil' pussy that just cut you off," he replied, snickering.

"Go to hell, Dank."

Chapter 10
Dank

After Totta skrted off on me, I was standing beside my car at my grandmother's crib laughing my ass off at him. The entire day with that fool had been a blast. From the time he woke up, Totta was one interesting and funny character. He kept complaining about Jonzella not answering her phone. As I thought about my homie complaining, he reminded me of a nagging fly. However, I knew how he was feeling. He wasn't alone; yet, I wasn't going to the lengths that he was.

"What you doing out here in this cold without a jacket on, Casey?" my grandmother asked as she slid out the side door.

"It's not that cold out here, Grandma," I chuckled as I enjoyed January's breezy weather.

"I don't want to hear anything about you being sick within the next couple of weeks," she fussed as she strolled towards me.

"I won't," I snickered before saying, "I got on two undershirts underneath this long sleeve, Grandma."

With a smile on her face, she said, "My boy."

Nodding my head, I looked at the woman that helped raise me. With her big eyes on me, she said, "Your father will be coming in today. I want y'all to make nice with each other. Life's too short for y'all to be carrying on the way that y'all are, Casey."

"I didn't cease the communication with him. He did. I'm not going to kiss anyone's behind, Grandma. He didn't like my choices in life, and I understand that; yet, he still could've been in my life. I don't have any hatred towards the guy. Just not going to take advice from a man that can't keep his family."

"What happened between your father and mother is none of your business. You are the child. So you will stay in a child's place, understood?" she stated sweetly, yet demandingly.

"Yes, ma'am," I replied respectfully before saying, "that murder charge against me, Totta, and Danzo is dropped."

Clapping her hands before hugging me, my grandmother thanked God. After she was done thanking the Man above, she told me to bow my head. Doing as she commanded, she prayed over me, followed by praying for Danzo and Totta. Soon as the prayer was over, I lifted my head and my eyes landed on a new model, white Silverado truck pulling onto my grandmother's curb.

"Who is that?" I asked myself more so than my grandmother. I hoped like hell it wasn't a junkie.

"Your parents," my grandmother replied.

"Oh," I voiced with a smirk on my face.

With my keys in my hand, I turned around to start the engine on my whip. Knowing damn well that my father was going to start some shit, I was going to disappear before he got me riled up.

"Where do you think you are going?" my grandmother and mother asked at the same time.

"Home. Got a slight headache," I replied, lying about the headache.

"Did you take something for it?" my mother asked seriously as she ambled towards me.

"Gloria, you can't tell when he's lying. Casey, don't have no damn headache. He's running from a possible argument with his father," my grandmother responded as she looked at me with a raised eyebrow.

"Hi, son," my father, Curtis Price, said casually as he strolled into my grandmother's yard.

"What's up?" I replied as I studied the man wearing a gray Ralph Lauren button-up shirt, white jeans, and a pair of gray, low top Ralph Lauren sneakers.

"Came down to spend some time with you," he voiced amiably as he extended his hand.

Putting my hand in his, we shook hands briefly before I shoved my hands in my pockets. It seemed as if everything in the neighborhood went quiet. Moments passed before anyone said anything.

Caught Up In A D-Boy's Illest Love 2

Ring. Ring. Ring.

"Whoever that is, Casey, they can wait. You and your father need to talk," my grandmother commanded.

Nodding my head, I pulled my cell phone out of my pocket. Seeing Jonsey's name on the screen, I thought, *To hell with what you saying, Grandma. This my lady.* With a huge smile on my face, my grandmother and mother had some slick shit to say.

"Well, that must be that young lady from Wal-Mart calling. Well, in that case, Curtis, y'all might talk a little later," my grandmother snickered.

Ignoring her comment, I answered the phone.

"Hi, beautiful," I cooed in the phone as my heart flipped several times.

"Hey. I don't know why I'm calling," she said quickly and oh so sweetly.

"Come on, my queen, you know why you are calling me. I hope you are telling me that you want to see me. We have a lot to talk about," I said casually as I stared at the ground, hoping she wasn't going to say anything that would put me in a sour mood.

"Casey, I...I don't think we should be friends anymore. I enjoyed my time with you. I...I...fuck!" she said lowly.

"Nawl, Jonsey, I ain't hearing that. Whatever you want to know I will tell you. I don't have anything to hide. A nigga need you, mane.

I don't see myself with nobody else," I begged, feeling myself getting angry.

"I don't see how we can be together. You are a street guy, and I'm not street, at all. Those two lifestyles don't mix. You are for killing people and destroying homes; whereas, I'm not with that."

"I'll leave the streets alone for you. Queen, I'll go legit for you," I blurted out.

As I spoke, my grandmother said, "Damn, she must got some powerful cat between her legs to make this nigga say he'll go legit." Her comment caused my parents to chuckle.

"Oh, my god, Casey, who said that?" Jonsey inquired before laughing.

With a stern face, I glared at my grandmother while answering Jonsey's question. "My no manners grandmother."

"Oh, wow. Ummm," Jonsey stated nervously.

"How about this...you tell me when can I see you?" I eagerly asked.

"Don't know, yet. Not sure if we are coming back," she shot back.

Not letting the comment piss me off, I said, "Okay, how about this...you tell me where you at, and I'll come to you."

After I made that statement, the sweet Jonsey disappeared.

"No, you stay your ass right where you are! You and Totta are the reasons why Jonzella and I are so damn distraught right now. I don't know what in the hell...you know, what fuck it. Our friendship is no longer acceptable in my eyes, and tell Totta to stop contacting my sister. She wants nothing to do with him as I don't want anything to do with you!"

Before I got a chance to speak my mind, Jonsey hung up the phone. Angrily growling as I rocked my neck from side to side, I tried calling her back—only to be sent to the voicemail. Ignoring the fact that my grandmother and parents were in my face, I shouted, "Fuck!"

Walking towards my car, I said, "I'll be back."

"Son, give her some time to cool off. The worst thing you can do is press the issue when she's thinking. Give her some time," my mother stated softly.

"I can't, Momma. If I give her too much time, she won't speak to me," I voiced in an unsteady breath.

"If you never listened to me, listen to me now...give her some space. Whatever y'all are going through she needs the time to think. Maybe she might come around or she won't, but at least you gave her free reign to weigh out the options of being with you."

Turning around to look at my mother's beautiful face, I said, "How do you know giving her time will help me?"

"I don't, but I do know this. If you keep pestering her, that will run her away. Just ask your father how I ran him away," she voiced sadly while looking at the man that was once her husband.

"But he cheated, so that doesn't help me," I huffed.

"In actuality, I cheated. I asked forgiveness, and he couldn't give it to me at the time. He needed his space to think, and I didn't give that to him. When your father was dealing with his current wife, him and I were separated."

"But y'all was still married ... so in actuality, he still was cheating, Momma," I replied, not giving the man no break.

"Off that subject, for now, give her some space," my mother voiced sternly as she gave me the 'don't fuck with me' facial expression.

"Okay. I'll be back," I stated blankly as I wasn't hearing what my mother was talking about.

"Son, why are you running from the talk that we must have?"

"Dad, there's nothing to talk about. I'm not in the right mind frame to talk," I told him as I didn't look at him.

"What about this murder charge you are facing?"

"Those charges are dropped," I voiced nonchalantly.

"Ahhh, that's great news. Did they choose not to use those two guys as witnesses?" my mother asked.

Turning around to face her, I said, "That and the fact that they are dead."

"Well, damn," the elders voiced as they kept their eyes on me, especially my grandmother.

"They aren't going to come after y'all for their deaths, are they?" my father asked.

Shaking my head in response to his question, I kept my eyes on my grandmother. From the look in her pretty peepers, I knew that she was thinking that my crew and I had something to do with it.

"Good," my father replied happily.

For the last time, I told them that I would be back. Hopping in my whip, I peeled away from their residence. Wanting to hang out with some fellas, I called Danzo. He told me that he and J-Money were over J-Money's crib. Telling me to come over, I jumped on the interstate, aiming for the East Side of Montgomery.

Fifteen minutes later, I was pulling into a secluded, exclusive neighborhood off Atlanta Highway. Cruising through the residential streets, I saw myself and Jonsey living in the neighborhood as we had two children playing in the front yard, us sitting on the porch as I rubbed her swollen belly. With a smile on my face, I knew that I had to make that daydream come true! I wasn't going to have it no other way.

Making a swift left turn into J-Money's driveway, I saw him and Danzo on the porch. Shutting off the engine, I slid out of the car, all the while saying, "What it do, fellas?"

"Coolin' my nigga, coolin'," they replied in unison.

"I feel ya," I responded as I strolled towards the porch.

"Where that fool Totta at?" J-Money laughed. The way he laughed let me know he heard about Totta and Momma Shirl.

Chuckling, I said, "Mane, that nigga at the crib. He had one eventful day."

"We heard," Danzo piped before shaking his head with a smile on his face.

"Miss Shirl, don't be playing about them damn cookies," J-Money voiced, snickering.

"Shit, nawl," Danzo and I replied in unison as I took a seat next to J-Money.

"I heard that y'all case is dismissed," J-Money voiced as he fired up a cigarette.

"Yep," I replied.

"I know y'all niggas glad."

"Damn, right," Danzo voiced excitedly.

Shooting the breeze with the fellas, the subject changed to the day we were in Myrtle Beach scoping out the guys. Danzo informed J-Money and me on how he overheard that the dudes had a sixty percent chance of surviving, and how he wanted them to have a zero chance of living.

"I'm chilling with the parents, pretending as if I'm waiting on a family member. In my mind, I decided that I should pretend to be a nurse. It took me a long ass minute to pull the shit off. Soon as I did, it was over with. Reading over their files, I learned that the niggas had head trauma and that they were allergic to Morphine. My crazy ass had to figure out how to keep them in a coma which would result in them dying. So, a nigga Googled his ass off. Not finding any concrete answer to solve the solution, a nigga began to pray heavily that someone would finish them niggas off. What I really wanted to do was punch them niggas all in they shits where nobody could see fist prints; however, with nurses and doctors floating in and out of their room, a brother couldn't do shit."

"Wait...wait...you telling us that you were willing to beat them niggas skull so that it could swell more? You telling me that you had a badge and couldn't swipe no damn narcotics to cardiac arrest them niggas?" I voiced lowly.

"Yep," he replied with a smile on his face.

Shaking my head, I said, "Well, damn. No argument my way. All I wanted was for them to be dead."

"But I did find something extremely odd when I went in the room and started scoping through a laptop in there," Danzo voiced.

"Why in the hell was you snooping in a damn laptop?" J-Money and I said in unison as we leaned forward.

"Mane, look, a nigga nosey, but anyways, I believe one of them dude's parents paid some niggas to knock them boys off."

Plopping my back against the chair, I stared at Danzo in disbelief. Shaking my head, I replied, "Anything is possible in today's world."

"True," J-Money said.

We became quiet as each of us went into our own little world. Moments passed before the fellas started rapping. Meanwhile, I was thinking about Jonsey. Wanting to think and beg her in peace, I dapped the fellas up and told them that I would holler at them later.

"We going to Club Magic tonight, you in?" J-Money inquired as I stepped off his porch.

"Yeah."

"We gon' discuss a little business. I'm about to revamp The Savage Clique. Baked and Ruger will be in attendance," J-Money voiced professionally.

"I'm in. The usual time?"

"Yeah."

"A'ight. Y'all niggas be easy."

"You too," they replied as I peeled to my car with my queen heavily on my mind.

***

At midnight, we strolled through Club Magic. As usual, it was packed to capacity. Bitches were in our faces, and I didn't crack a smile, give out a hug, or none of that shit. I wasn't in the mood for any of them. I had my mind on one woman, and it was going to stay that way.

As we made our way to the back of the club, a cold hand found its way towards my wrist. Turning around as I shook the hand away, I stared Diamond in the face. Soon as she placed a smile on her face,

I walked off. Shortly afterwards, she pulled me close to her and whispered in my ear, "We have some unfinished business, Dank."

Not the one to be played with, I shook her off me. Glaring in her dark-skinned face, I slowly mouthed, "Stay the fuck away from me."

Making sure that there weren't going to be anymore issues between the two of us, I made my way to the back of the club. Soon as I spotted J-Money, Danzo, Baked, and Ruger, I knew things were about to kick off. Approaching the fellas, they started laughing. With the music blasting and a confused facial expression, I shrugged my shoulders and mouthed, "What?"

They pointed behind me. Turning around to see what they were pointing at, I grew agitated. *Why won't she leave me alone?* Ignoring the broad, I dapped them up. After we scanned the dance floor and the VIP section, we made our way to The Savage Clique's sixth place of business. Stepping in the far back of the club, J-Money began to talk.

"This meeting is about taking over Baymatch's territory. Danzo or Dank, do y'all want it?" J-Money inquired.

I shook my head, whereas Danzo nodded his.

"Dank, what is your position in the game?" J-Money asked professionally.

"I'm thinking of exiting it and going legit," I told him honestly.

"What's up with you and Chief wanting to get out the game?" Baked asked curiously as he fired up a cigarette.

"It gets old. I have enough money stashed back where I can do whatever I want to do. Y'all really think X going to leave the game behind?"

Everybody nodded their head minus Danzo.

"Honestly, I think it's time for her to exit the game. She's been in the streets since she was fourteen years old. The streets is no place for a pregnant woman of X's caliber. She deserves to be laid back while raising her child. She's not only a savage but a sweet and caring individual," Ruger voiced passionately about their chief.

"If I didn't know any better, Ruger, I would say that you are soft on X," Danzo laughed.

"Not at all. She's like a sister to me," he replied as his creepy, dark eyes roamed over Danzo.

Another hour of discussing business, and we were leaving the back of the club. By the time we made it to the dance floor, The Savage Clique ran out of the club.

Danzo and I looked at each other, shrugged our shoulders, and said, "I wonder who X don' killed now."

Not feeling the club but knowing it was the best place for me at the moment, I decided to hang out with Danzo. The partygoers were enjoying their time; whereas, I was just there, spending unnecessary money. I saw a female shaped like Jonsey, and my mind went crazy. Thinking of the one woman that had my mind in an uproar, I pulled out my phone and sent her a text.

Me: *Jonsey, I don't want to be apart from you. A nigga just want to love you. Please, don't shut down on me. Call me soon as you read this.*

Holding my phone in my hand, I prayed heavily that she would call me. Five minutes turned into ten minutes, and before I knew it, twenty minutes had passed by, and Jonsey hadn't reached out to me. Looking like a sad puppy, I told Danzo that I would holler at him later. After dapping him up, I waltzed out of Club Magic with my head held high, but my spirit was lower than a motherfucker.

God, don't let her slip out of my life. I need her, I thought as I ambled towards my car.

Chapter 11
Jonzella

I haven't gotten an ounce of sleep since we left the hospital yesterday. Between the blowup between our parents, the sickness, Totta contacting me via different Facebook pages, and Jonsey worried about what she should do about Casey, I was one distraught female.

I was the first one woke this morning, so I waltzed outside with my favorite green blanket, which Totta bought me, wrapped around my body. Sitting on the back porch with a cup of lukewarm ginger ale, I enjoyed the cold air. The sun was non-existent. The weather matched my mood—muggy. As I slipped into a world of my own, I began to feel bad for Mom. She didn't deserve the things that Daddy put her through.

Ever since I was a little child, I would see my Renee and Jonsey's dad together. Several times, I told Renee to stay away from him. Every time, she would laugh in my face and told me to be thankful that they took me in. In a young child's mind, I didn't understand why she said that. However, as a grown woman, I believed I knew exactly what she meant.

"What are you doing up so early?" Dad asked as he stretched his long arms.

"Couldn't sleep," I replied quietly as I zoned into a red gnome.

"Is the ginger ale calming your stomach?" he inquired, taking a seat next to me.

"Not really," I responded before taking a sip of the soda.

"Jonzella, are you pregnant?" he blurted out in a low timbre as he glanced at me.

Not sure if I should answer the question, I quickly remembered that I never lied to him since he legally made me his daughter. Thus, I didn't see the need in me lying to him now. Slowly nodding my head, I sighed as the tears flooded my face.

"I knew the moment I placed my eyes on you," he chuckled lightly.

"Are you disappointed in me?" I questioned while wiping my eyes.

"Not at all," he voiced sincerely before continuing, "As long as you know how to juggle your studies, perfect health management, and my grandchild, we will be absolutely fine. Does the father know?"

Nodding my head, I remained quiet because I knew if I said anything else, Daddy would go berserk.

"He's willing to do his part correct?"

"Yes."

"Good. When will I get a chance to meet him?" Daddy continued.

"When the baby is born."

"Why so long, Jonzella?"

Shrugging my shoulders, I exhaled sharply. Daddy became quiet, and I was very thankful for that. I didn't want him knowing the things that I did. It was best that I left him wondering why I didn't want him meeting Totta.

"Can we keep my pregnancy quiet for a while, please?" I asked as I looked into his loving eyes.

"As long as your body will allow you to, we will keep it a promise," he voiced sweetly as he held up his pinky finger.

Laughing until happy tears streamed down my face, I shook my head and held out my pinky finger, followed by us saying, "Pinky swear."

Simmering the laughter down, I was ready to ask him a question that I knew would put me in a grown up's place with him.

Sighing heavily several times, I finally got the balls to say, "Why did you sleep with Renee? Was it a bargaining chip between the two of you?"

Taking his time answering the question, I didn't know what he was going to say; however, I knew I had to brace my mental for whatever came out of his mouth.

"Are you sure you are ready for this talk?" Daddy asked me seriously as he looked me in my eyes.

"I am," I heard myself say.

"Well, umm...Renee and I grew up together. I was the first one that took her virginity as well as she was the first one that took mine. I was in love with your mother when we were younger, yet she had ways that I couldn't see myself dealing with on a daily basis. When I learned of her pregnancy, I didn't know if you were mine or the dude she was dating at the time. Knowing that she could be carrying my child, I made sure that she was in the same city as me."

With raised eyebrows, I was at a loss of words. That didn't stop him from continuing to talk.

"To this day, I don't know if you are biologically mine or not ... and honestly, I don't give a damn. That's just how much I love your mother."

"Do you love Mom?"

"I do, but it's a different type of love. I don't love her the same way I love Renee. I had to marry Venette because she was better for me. She is what people considered a good woman."

"Then why continue to deal with Renee?" I asked in a confused manner.

Shrugging his shoulders, he sighed, "I guess Daddy just have a thing for bad girls."

With his comment lingering in the air, I thought, *Like Daddy, like daughter.*

Silence overcame us as we enjoyed the morning air with me snuggled in his arms. I didn't care if he was my biological father or not, I still loved him the same.

***

"I know you are resting, but can you please help a sister out?" Jonsey begged as I slept.

"What's up?" I replied groggily as I never opened my eyes.

"I don't know what to do about Casey. He's all through my mental."

"I can't help you when I'm in the same boat myself, sis," I replied seriously as I opened my eyes.

"Your situation is different...it involves a child. So, you have no choice but to communicate with him," she huffed lowly before getting underneath my covers.

"I don't have to talk to him because of the pregnancy."

"That's wrong of you if you don't converse with him on the well-being of the baby, Jonzella. I know what he said was hurtful, but I—" she began to say before I cut her off.

"Off that subject, are there any updates on the funeral arrangements," I voiced, not in the mood to think about my current situation with Totta.

"Tomorrow," Jonsey voiced quickly.

With a raised eyebrow, I said, "Why so early and on a Sunday?"

"According to Mom, Dad and her started making plans for the funeral the day they called us with the news of Kevin and Kenny not making it."

Taking a moment before I said anything, I stared at Jonsey as if she was crazy. I didn't think they would have the funeral so soon. I wasn't ready to go back to Alabama.

"Are you wanting to get out of the house? I want to shop?" Jonsey asked sweetly.

"Not really, but since I know it's therapy for you…I will go," I voiced lovingly as I softly smiled in her face.

"Be ready in thirty minutes," she spat happily before hopping up and down on the bed.

"Don't do that!" I yelled.

Covering her mouth as she giggled, Jonsey replied with, "Sorry, sis. Forgot."

With a smirk on my face, I said, "Where are Mom and Dad?"

"Gone."

Knowing that key information, I informed her about me telling Daddy about the pregnancy. I decided to keep his true feelings and history with Renee amongst him and me. The less Jonsey knew the better. I wasn't going to have a wedge driven with my best-friend turned sister. I didn't want her to view me any differently.

After our conversation, she said, "You learned of your doctor's appointment. Now, do the right thing and let Totta know. It's okay if you don't want to be bothered with him, relationship wise. However, give him the right to be there for his child, regardless of what he said."

Snatching my phone from underneath the pillow, I dialed Totta's number. On the third ring, he excitedly answered the phone by saying, "My queen."

Sighing heavily, I said, "Umm. I'm just calling to inform you that the doctor's appointment is scheduled for February 2nd at ten. I'll call you closer to the time frame with the location and a reminder."

"Okay," he quickly voiced lightly before continuing. "I'm sorry that I said those hurtful things to you. I was on some more shit. Do you forgive me?"

"Yeah, Totta...um, well, I was just calling you to inform you...I gotta go," I sighed, not wanting to get off the phone with him.

"Please don't hang up, Jonzella. A nigga misses you. Real nigga shit, I'm going crazy without you, mane," he sighed sharply.

With a smile on my face, I didn't respond. My heart was fluttering as I rehashed him saying that he's going crazy without me. Meanwhile, he had a whole bulldagger harassing me about him.

"Jonzella?" Totta spoke louder, interrupting my thoughts.

"Yeah?" I questioned quietly.

"Did you hear what I said about missing you?"

"Yeah."

"So, you don't miss me?" he voiced, sounding like a wounded dog.

"Totta, look, I didn't call you to try to get us back together. I just wanted to do the right thing by the baby and that's to keep you in the loop," I voiced not as confident as I wanted.

"I'm not hearing that noise you talking about. I want...fuck...I need you in my life. Our child will not be in a one parent home. That was not my plan, Jonzella Brown," he announced angrily.

Not in the mood for his tantrum, I spat, "Well, you should've watched your damn mouth. I guess the conversation I was bringing up touched your soul a little too much. But anyways, like I said, I was just reaching out to you so that you know when my first appointment is. I got stuff to do, so I'll see you on that date."

Not giving him time to respond, I ended the call. Flopping back on the bed, I was one confused person. I wanted Totta in my life, but I didn't know if it was the right thing to do given that him and Dank were the reasons why we were burying my brothers.

Getting off the bed, I prayed sincerely and heavily that God led me in the right direction.

Chapter 12
Totta

"Boy, what's wrong with you?" Momma asked as she took a seat next to me.

"Nothing," I lied as my eyes were glued to the TV.

"You been at my house since eleven o'clock this morning looking foolish. After you got off the phone two hours ago, you sho' nuff been looking dumb and lost. So, lie to me one more time, and I'mma pop you upside your head," she sternly said while glaring into my face.

Sighing heavily, but not to the point I was being disrespectful, I rubbed my hands together, followed by saying, "I made a mistake, Momma. I messed around and said some foul ish to a chick I'm digging."

"Wait a whole minute...Totta got feelings for a broad!" Gigi, my baby sister, shouted before laughing. Her comment caused our other sister, Nedra, to stroll in the living room with Gigi in tow, followed by Gigi turning down the TV before taking a seat next to Momma.

Chuckling, our mother said, "Now, Gigi, why did you turn the TV down so low?"

"Momma, I gots to hear what this fool of a brother has to say about a female he actually cares about," she voiced as she gave me her full attention.

Growing annoyed with them, I said, "Y'all two get on my nerves. I swear y'all act like y'all are teenagers instead of in y'all twenties."

Smacking their mouths as momma said, "What's wrong, Totta?"

"I'm trying to figure out how I'm going to get myself out of the mess I created."

"You must've got her pregnant?" Nedra huffed with an ugly look on her face.

Always up for free, helpful advice, I wasn't sure if I should tell the entire story of how I fucked up. That would include me telling them about the murder charges my crew and I were facing. Staying on the outskirts was the safest route for me.

"Umm, so is that the problem... the chick pregnant and you don't want it?" Gigi questioned with a smirk on her face.

"Her being pregnant isn't the issue...it's what I did and said to her prior to learning that she was pregnant. Not to mention, what I didn't say after learning that she was pregnant," I confessed as I fumbled with my hands while looking at my mother's cleaned black carpet.

"What did you say and do to her, Totta?" Momma inquired curiously.

"I really don't want to get into the specifics of things. I need to know how to make it right, so she won't shove me out...like I asked her to do."

My sisters shook their heads and asked in unison, "Why would you tell her that?"

"Because I was being an asshole. She was on a sensitive subject, and I was trying to escape that conversation. When I hopped out of her bed, she was crying and saying things that made me think...well, over think. I got mad, put my clothes on, and proceeded to her room door. She threw something at me. Not caring what it was, I ran back to the bed and hemmed her up."

"You did what!" my mother yelled instead of asking.

Damn near jumping in Nedra's lap, I quickly said, "I snatched her by her hair, followed by putting my hands around her neck. I didn't apply any pressure. I just let her know not to throw anything at me. I didn't hit her, Momma, I swear."

"What did she throw at you?" Momma asked with an attitude.

"A pregnancy test," I said, looking sad.

"So, you telling us that you showed your ass because she threw a pregnancy test at you?" Nedra laughed while shaking her head.

Ignoring her question, I bit down on the inside of my bottom lip. I was a lost soul, and they weren't helping me out at all.

"Did you know it was a pregnancy test before you went crazy?" Gigi inquired.

"Nope."

"What did you say once you learned what it was and what it said?" Momma probed.

Hesitating on answering her question, I said a series of 'um's' before she shouted her question again.

Bowing my head, I replied lowly, "Nice knowing you."

The loud wows that left the women's mouths had me scared to look at our mother. Hearing their reaction made me feel more of an asshole than I already knew I was. Several minutes passed before anyone said anything. Stealing glances at our mother, I saw that she was extremely disappointed in me.

"Momma, please say something. How do I make things right?" I begged with pleading eyes.

"Before I answer your question, I need to know how in the hell did y'all arrive at the part where you were trying to escape...I want full details, Joshua Nixon," Momma announced sternly.

Huffing, I said, "That's not important."

"Yes, it is."

"No, it's not, Momma."

"Lil' boy, I know you better than you know yourself. In order for any female to say they are pregnant by you, you have to care for them. You have never had a female that said they were pregnant for you. I've never had to worry about scheming ass females popping up at my door with the nonsense. Y'all were having a serious discussion that scared you shitless. Now, what was it!"

Before I spoke, I fired up a cigarette. Taking three pulls of the nicotine stick, I told them everything. By the time I was finished, all three said, "Well, damn."

"Now, will y'all help me get my queen and seed back," I begged while looking into each of their faces.

"Jonzella loves you, Totta. For a woman to tell you to use her instead of killing her brothers...got some mad, raw love for you. Then, for you to say it was nice knowing you after you learned of her being pregnant is a hurtful thing, son. Trust, I know. Your father did me the same way. Shit, damn near crushed me," Momma said in a mellow tone.

"Bro, all I can tell you to do is fight for her," Gigi replied sincerely.

Nodding my head at Gigi's comment, I turned my head to Nedra and said, "What should I do?"

"Bro, I'mma be honest with you...I don't know. You in a crazy situation. She's dealing with the burial of her brothers, who were the same niggas that could've testified against you. Then you say some dumb ish when you learn that she's carrying your seed. I really don't know what to tell you."

Not feeling any better by Nedra's comment, I turned my head to momma and stared at her. Firing up a cigarette and inhaling, she shook her head at me.

"Come on with it, Momma. I'm a big boy. I can take it," I voiced in an untruthful timbre.

"Have you talked since the incident?" Gigi asked.

"She called me today."

"And?" they said in unison.

"She told me when the doctor's appointment is."

"And that was all she said? Any laughing or asking how you are doing?" My mother said.

"She was real blunt with what she had to say. No asking me how I was doing."

"Boy, I'on know what to tell you. I will be able to read her better once I meet her. When is the doctor's appointment?" Momma questioned.

"February 2nd."

"I'll cook dinner. Bring her over."

"Okay."

"In the meantime, you better do all you can to make things right," Gigi stated seriously as she hopped off the floor.

Ring. Ring. Ring.

Soon as I pulled my phone out of my left pocket, my eyes grew big as the smile on my face was bigger. I proudly answered the phone as my sister and mother stared into my face.

"Hello," I voiced in my baritone voice.

Caught Up In A D-Boy's Illest Love 2

"Hey. I don't care if we are in a relationship or not, but I don't want my child fatherless. I don't need you playing mind games with me. I'm not the type of female that is bitter because her baby daddy doesn't want her. I just want a normal, respectable co-parentship between us. All that I ask is that you don't have any hoodrats around my baby, and I won't have any random nigga around our child."

Hearing her saying something about a random nigga around our child, caused me to forget that my sister and mother were in the room.

"Jonzella, you must be out of your mind if you think I'mma have any random broads around my child, and you sure as hell ain't going to be dating no nigga. I'm the only nigga that's going to be renting to own that pussy."

As Jonzella laughed so did my goofy, stupid ass sisters; meanwhile, our momma chuckled, "Milord, this boy here stupid as hell."

Hopping away from the sofa, I ambled towards the kitchen where I could talk to my queen in peace. Leaving the living room did me no good as the women followed behind me. Sighing heavily, I told my family to chill so that I could talk in peace. Instead they yelled, "Nope. Now, tell Jonzella we said hey, and congratulations on the pregnancy."

"You heard my sisters and momma?" I asked.

"Yeah. Tell them hello and thank you," Jonzella said sweetly.

Relaying the message, I conversed with her like I did the first night I met her. I made sure to inquire about her eating habits and was she still vomiting. Learning that my little one was not acting up so much, I was thankful. As we lightly laughed and chatted, I wasn't sure how things would turn out for us, I prayed that I was on the right track of her forgiving me. I wanted to ask how her family was doing, but I knew that would stir up some feelings that I knew she was trying to escape.

Being the man that I was, I said, "Can I come up and comfort you in your time of need?"

Hesitating before answering, she quickly replied, "No. I think its best that you stay where you are. We are good on this front. Totta, it was nice talking to you in that old way, again."

"What exactly does that mean?"

"Just that it felt good talking to you as if we were on better terms, you know."

Nodding my head, I didn't know what to think. I had to see what was on her mind; however, I didn't know the right way of asking it.

"If there is anything that you want to know, I promise you I'll tell you. I'm not going to lie about anything, queen. What do you want to know?" I questioned honestly. I was done running from her. If she wanted to know what I had planned for her brothers, I was going to tell her the truth.

Sighing sharply, she said, "At this point and the futures, there's nothing that I want or need to know. I'm done asking questions. I'm done pondering about us, what was going to happen to us, and what led you to...anyways, if it's not about the baby, I won't call you, and you should be the same way."

Not liking her answer, I angrily spat, "Mane, why it gotta be like?"

"You were digging in me raw at the same time you was digging in another broad without a condom. Not to mention, I'm grieving my brothers' death," was all that she could say to keep me from going any further.

"Okay. Are you sure that all you want is for us to co-parent?" I asked through clenched teeth.

"Yes," she said without a moment's hesitation.

"You got it. So, um, text me the location and time of the doctor's appointment, and I'll be there," I told her as I felt tears welling in my eyes.

"Okay. Have a good one, Totta," she stated lowly.

"You, too," I said as I took the phone away from my ear.

The tears dropped, and before I knew it, I slung that motherfucking phone of mine against my mother's beautifully decorated kitchen tiled wall, all the while screaming, "Fuck!"

"Gigi and Nedra, it's been a long time since we have seen Totta like this...I think we need to give him some space," our mother said soothingly.

"Okay," they replied in unison as I placed my head on the refrigerator.

"I got faith that she's going to come back to you, big brother. I love you," Gigi said softly as she quickly hugged me before peeling away from me.

Not wanting them to see me at my weakest point, I couldn't stop the tears from falling. I couldn't stop the images of how frightened my queen looked when I snatched her hair, followed by putting my hands around her neck, and I surely couldn't stop the sobs of saying that I was sorry.

"I don't want nobody else but her. How am I gonna get her back, mane?" I cried as I felt like a little whiny bitch.

I don't know how long I was in the kitchen crying for my mistakes against the woman that I knew I had deep feelings for. All I knew was that my homie was standing to the right of me.

"All I gotta say is that we gonna get our queens back...by any means necessary," Dank spoke sincerely as he handed me a napkin.

Chapter 13
Jonsey

Sunday, January 22ⁿᵈ

Yesterday was so sad and painful to witness. The wails from my mother sent ripples of chills through my body. It was to a point that my father couldn't control my mother's outburst. There was nothing that we could say to calm her. The worst part of saying our final goodbyes to Kevin and Kenny was the fact that Jonzella and I were deeply caring for the guys that were responsible for their death.

At the repast, Jonzella and I served our guests as quietly as we could. If I was in my thoughts about Casey, I knew that Jonzella was in the zone thinking about Totta. We were in one hell of a jam. Neither of us talked about the guys, yet it was apparent that we missed them something awful.

I read every text message and listened to every voicemail that Casey left me. Each time I wanted to call him. I needed to hear his voice. I had questions that I wanted answered, yet, when I was looking at the call button, I couldn't press the damn thing. I couldn't lie as if I didn't want to be with him because I did; yet, I knew the truth was causing a terrible heartache, which I couldn't shake. I prayed that I would get over him quickly, but given that I had a crush on him for three years and had the pleasure of being in his loving presence, it was going to be a great task for me.

"Jonsey and Jonzella," our father called out.

Coming out of my thinking zone with my eyes planted on the large, platinum lion, I said, "Yes, sir."

"You ladies have quite a trip ahead of y'all. I think it's safe to say that y'all can pack up and head back home. Your mother will be fine. I'm sure y'all will miss school tomorrow. However, Wednesday, y'all behinds better be in class," he voiced sweetly yet demandingly.

"Yes, sir," we replied in unison before leaving standing to our feet.

"Girls," our father called out, causing us to turn around.

"Yes, sir."

"I'm so proud of you two. I don't know what I would've done without you two being present. Even though I'm not talking to Kyvin, I highly believe y'all should reach out to him. At the end of the day, he is still your brother."

"I tried to call him, but he sent me to voicemail. I've sent him numerous texts, and he hasn't replied to any of them," Jonzella lightly voiced.

"Okay," our father stated, blankly.

I, on the other hand, wasn't going to reach out to his disrespectful, hating ass. He was the oldest, acting like a little child.

Always wanting someone in trouble because of who he is. I could give a care less about him being in his funky attitude.

Ten minutes later, Jonzella and I were fully packed. Sliding down the stairs two at a time, I was eager to get out of the depressing house. The life that Kenny and Kevin brought to the home was forever gone. My mother yelling at them to calm down was never going to exist again. Jonzella and Kenny fighting about food would never happen again. Kevin and I fighting over small things were forever gone. If I was tired of crying, I knew that everyone else was.

Before leaving the home, we made sure to shower our mother with kisses, hugs, and I love you's. Soon as we stepped out of the door, I noticed a black van with tinted windows parked across the street. With a frown on my face, I thought *I know damn well them niggas ain't up here scoping out our parents.*

"Jonzella, do you see that van?" I asked in a low tone as our father shouted for us to stop.

Doing as he commanded, followed by turning around to face him, Jonzella replied, "Yeah, I see it."

Daddy quickly approached us with his arms outstretched. Falling into them, he made sure to tell us how much he loved us. Saying that we loved him also, he voiced, "Jonzella, make sure you make your doctor's appointment to check on the health of my grandbaby."

"I already did. It's on February 2," she responded lowly before placing a kiss on his left cheek.

"My girl. Your secret is safe with me. I'll let you tell your mother whenever you are ready. Okay?"

"Okay," she replied.

Peeling away from us, he nodded his head for us to carry on.

"I'll drive, Jonsey. You been chauffeuring me around long enough," Jonzella joked as she waltzed to the trunk.

"Do you think the guys are in that van?" I asked quietly while trying to keep my eyes off the mysterious vehicle.

"Who knows with them niggas," she voiced nonchalantly as she extended her hand.

Knowing what she wanted, I gently dropped the keys in her palms. Before getting in the car, we waved at our father. Starting the engine, Jonzella selected one of her and our deceased brothers' favorite music albums. "Focus" by U.S.D.A. played at a low decibel.

"This is for y'all, Kenny and Kevin. I'm really going to miss y'all," she voiced sadly as she turned the volume up.

Buckling up, Jonzella bobbed along to the beat of the song as she reversed out of our parents' driveway. Quickly looking at the van, I rolled my eyes as hard as I could. In a matter of minutes, Jonzella whipped my vehicle on I-20 W. Looking at the clock, it stated that it was 1:02 p.m. Knowing that we weren't going to touch down in Montgomery until nine or so at night, I kicked off my shoes, reclined the seat back, and let the beat of "White Girl" bump my back.

My phone vibrated, causing me to pull it out of my pants pocket. Seeing Casey's name on the notification bar, I tapped on it. Soon as his message opened, I read it. The things he was saying had a sister wanting to tear up. Having the need to respond, I didn't. Reading his message two more times, I turned down the radio and said, "Jonzella, I want to talk to him so bad."

"Then, talk to him, Jonsey," she replied, not looking at me.

"But it feels so wrong," I whined.

"Look, I'm not finna deal with you and all that damn whining now. Either you going to talk to the man or not. You are not going to work my nerves for the next seven hours and some odd minutes about that man, Jonsey. So, make a decision. Whatever you choose, I'm behind you one thousand percent," she voiced in an agitated timbre.

"Okay," I replied with a smirk on my face.

Choosing not to reach out, I sat back. In need of something to drink, I reached underneath the seat and pulled out a bottle of E&J that I took out of Daddy's liquor cabinet, the first night we arrived in South Carolina. As I popped the cap on the bottle, Jonzella's laughing ass turned down the radio and said, "Whoa, you drinking without me?"

Chuckling, I spat, "Sure is. No drinking for your pregnant ass!"

"Ooouu, you didn't have to do me like that. I'm so in need of a drink," she cooed as she briefly watched me down half of the bottle.

"Now, I can sit back and shut the fuck up. My mind will be occupied by enjoying the scenery and music," I voiced to myself more so than to my sister.

"We gon' be just fine," she voiced in a not so confident tone.

***

At nine thirty p.m., Jonzella was pulling into our grassy driveway. A sister was glad to be at home. My nasty thoughts for the past five hours had me eager to get home. The liquor had a way of making me become mellow, yet horny, at the same time. As we traveled through Georgia, I had it set in my mind that I was going to pop up at Casey's house, demand the dick, and then go back home.

Shutting off the engine, Jonzella said, "I think I want to visit the Shack on Atlanta Highway, you in?"

"No," I replied as I opened the door. Instantly, a cold rush of air surrounded me. Shouting the word shit loudly, I ran to the door. I was on a mission and standing in the cold was starting to ruin that.

Hopping out of the car laughing while taking her precious time walking to our porch, Jonzella didn't know she was on the brinks of getting cursed out. Annoyed at her speed level, I impatiently said, "Can you hurry the fuck up? It's cold out here."

"Don't rush me. You should've put on your jacket," she laughed as she climbed the four steps at a snail's pace.

Snatching the keys out of her hand, I quickly opened the door. Stepped into our warm, cozy establishment and a sigh of relief escaped my mouth. Closing the door behind her, Jonzella said, "Home, sweet, home."

Running to the bathroom, I turned on the water. Peeling out of my shoes, I ran to my room. In three minutes, I had my clothes laid on the bed. Gliding to the closet, I retrieved a pair of white sneakers. Placing them at the foot of my bed, Jonzella stood at the door with a raised eyebrow. Taking off my clothes, I said, "Why are you staring at me like that?"

"You ain't going to The Shack with me...so, where are you going?" she asked with a quizzical facial expression.

"To fuck, and then I'll be back home," I replied blankly.

"Well, damn. Um, have a great time then, Miss I'm On That Liquor," she chuckled as I bypassed her.

Thirty minutes of being in the shower, I hopped out ready to tackle the man that made me feel better on the inside. Running to my room to get dressed, the doorbell sounded off. Coming to a complete stop, I wondered who was at the door. Thinking that Jonzella was going to answer the door, I was wrong. The doorbell sounded off again, followed by several loud knocks on the door.

"Who is it?" I asked as I slipped on my pants and shirt.

"Casey."

What the hell? I was supposed to be popping up at his spot, I thought as I ran to the door.

Happily saying, "Hold on."

"Okay," he voiced patiently.

Unlocking and opening the door, the chocolate god was standing in my face. That man looked so damn delicious to the point I quickly snatched his ass inside. Aggressively pressing him against the front door's baseboard, I parted his mouth with my tongue. As I gave him the kiss I had been so longing to do, Casey picked me up followed by closing the door with his foot.

Removing my mouth from his, I said, "I was on the way to your house."

"Is that where you wanna be?" he inquired as he stopped at the end of the sofa.

Nodding my head while gazing into his eyes, Casey voiced, "Are you sure?"

"Absolutely," I voiced as Jonzella strolled out of her room.

"What's up, Jonzella? How are you?"

"Good, and you?" she quickly replied as she bypassed us, ambling towards the kitchen.

"Great, now that y'all are back in town. Jonzella, this is the first and last time that I'm going to get in you and Totta's business.

Please reach out to him; I've never seen him in such a bad place. Can you please do that for me?" Casey begged in a pleading timbre.

Sighing heavily, Jonzella responded with, "I already talked to Totta. He knows what's up. I'm not going to keep him out of our child's life. I'm not built like that."

"Okay," Casey replied before looking at me and saying, "You need shoes and a jacket, right?"

"Toothbrush, extra panties, and all that shit," I chuckled as I climbed off him.

Before I walked off, he turned me around and glared into my eyes. Shaking his head with a disappointed facial expression, Casey stated, "I think you should stay at home. I'mma holla at cha tomorrow when you are sober."

Looking at Casey as if I wanted to punch his face in, with an attitude I spat "Why?"

"Because you've been drinking. This isn't the Jonsey that I want. I want the sober Jonsey. Until she returns, then I don't want us to do anything that will cause the sober you to regret it," he voiced as he backed away.

Hearing him say all of that unnecessary bullshit caused my mind to shout a thousand curse words. Angry with him, I knew that we were going to get in a massive argument. I wanted the dick, and yet, he was trying to refuse me of having it because I'd been drinking—oh, hell no, I wasn't having that!

Caught Up In A D-Boy's Illest Love 2

With a smirk on my face, I spat, "Either you are going to fuck me, or I'm going to have a one-night stand with someone else."

Seeing a facial expression that I didn't recognize, I fed off it. My mouth became reckless as Jonzella came to Casey's aid. Not giving a damn about her telling me to calm down, I knew my statement would send Casey into insane mode.

"Oh, so you can orchestrate to murder our brothers, yet, you don't wanna fuck me because I've been drinking. Bet dat, my nigga! See will you like me running my pussy up and down another nigga's dick!" I spat nastily as I glared at him while he was making his way towards me.

Chapter 14
Dank

The entire way to my crib, Jonsey's mouth was going ninety miles per hour. Wanting to scream for her to shut the fuck up, I decided against it. I knew that she was hurting. I knew what she wanted. Against my better judgement, I was going to give her little ass just what she was seeking!

Strolling into my home with Jonsey over my shoulder, she was still talking shit. After I put in my security code, followed by locking the door, I shut off the lights that were on downstairs. Quickly creeping up the stairs, I was anxious to get her mouth on a different level. Upon reaching my bedroom, I flipped the light switch.

As I put Jonsey down, I nastily said, "Strip out of your fucking clothes and get on the bed."

Doing as I commanded, a brother had to shake his head. I didn't want to have sex with her given the state she was in. I knew that there was going to be some bullshit once she woke up in the morning. Yet, I couldn't stand the thought of another nigga satisfying her cravings.

Coming out of my clothes, I wanted to start my own rants; instead, I was going to rant in a way that was going to leave her sore for days to come. Strolling towards her naked body, I didn't say a word to her as I savagely shoved her legs on my shoulders before ramming my dick inside of her.

"Shitt," she cooed as she tried to sit up in the bed.

"Nawl, don't run from the dick, Jonsey. This is what you wanted, remember? You gonna take it how the fuck I serve it!" I growled as I maneuvered around her pussy as if she was just a broad giving me a nut. I was angry with her, and she was going to learn when to simmer down. She was going to learn that I was the Alpha, and what I said goes.

I thought by me giving her the dick in such a disrespectful manner, she would come to her senses and beg me to stop fucking her so harshly. That heifer shocked me when she started matching my swerving, fast deep thrusts. Enjoying how I was pleasing her inner part, Jonsey pulled me closer to her and stuck her tongue so far down my mouth to the point I started gagging.

"Ooouu, Casssey," she cooed as I continued slamming my man inside of her, trying to break what she was trying to do to me.

Alternating between slow and fast grinding on my dick, Jonsey had a nigga's toes curled to the max. Dropping my head beside hers, I bucked my eyes as I silently kept saying shit. I couldn't serve her my loving in a punishing type of way because the heifer overpowered me. She was on bottom and was fucking the shit out of me! A nigga was truly loss for word.

Caught Up In A D-Boy's Illest Love 2

On the brinks of releasing a much-needed nut and a manly groan, I had to gain control over the situation. There was no way in hell I was going to let Jonsey fuck me into submission. She would not be able to run back to Jonzella and tell her that she had me moaning like a little bitch.

Taking Jonsey's legs off my shoulders, I lifted off her body while spreading her legs wider. Glared into her beautiful brown eyes, I started making love to her. That was the only way to get her into submission. Slowly, yet eagerly, pushing my dick to the left corner of her hot spot, I tongue kissed my lady so passionately and lovingly.

"I feel some type of way about you, Casey, and it's not a bad feeling," she whined sweetly as her body began to shake. Knowing what was about to happen, I went the extra mile to grind in that one spot that was going to make her listen to me.

"Ahhhhh! Oh, my god! I'm finna nut, Cassseyy!" she yelled, loudly.

"Then do it," I growled while sucking on her neck.

Before the word it left my mouth, Jonsey creamed while continuing to call my name. Satisfied with the state she was in, I stared into her eyes. Biting down on her bottom lip, I stopped her by sliding my tongue across them.

Knowing that I had some things on my chest that she needed to hear, I briefly kissed her before saying, "I'm sick of playing with you. Yes, I was going to murder your brothers. They were going to take me away from you. I couldn't have that. Yes, I scoped out your parent's crib. Yes, I was there the day your brothers were shot, and no, I didn't send out the hit. Your brothers' death was not because of me and Totta. Somebody else already had it out for them. I need you to believe me, Jonsey. A nigga can't lose you over some shit that I didn't do, even though I planned to do it."

Ignoring what I said, she whined as her face frowned, indicating another orgasm she was on the brinks of having. Pissed that she didn't respond to what I had to say, I started stabbing her guts.

"Did...you...hear...me?" I asked. Each time I said a word, I went deeper inside of her.

Eyes rolling in the back of her head, she didn't say a word—only looked at me with a sex-crazed facial expression. Seeing that I was getting nowhere with her in the current state that she was in, I realized that she wasn't going home no time soon. Trying to get back into beast mode, I couldn't. Jonsey was on a different path, and I didn't know how to get control of the situation. My body was doing shit it had never done with any female I had fucked with.

"Fuckkk, what are you trying to do to me, girl?" I groaned as Jonsey's muscles clenched my dick so tightly.

"Fuck you good; then, go home and never talk to you again," she spat as she was back on the dominant role.

We were stubborn as hell in that bed. I didn't know what type of liquor she was on, but I was no match for her. The first four rounds, Jonsey won hands down. After each round, she wanted me to take her home. I wasn't hearing that at all. Thus, I created that fire inside of her again. Round five, I put my emotions to the side and fucked her as if she was just an ordinary bitch in the streets. I had her ass, and I didn't let up on her, no matter how she begged and pleaded for me to stop.

"Don't you fucking nut in me, Casey," she whined as her pussy became sloppy wet, followed by her moaning loudly as her body violently shook. That was the reaction I was waiting for since I had her in my bed.

"I do what I want," I said nonchalantly.

"You heard what the fuck I said," Jonsey popped off with an attitude.

Not liking the way she talked to me, I removed my penis and flipped her ass on her stomach. Doing the absolute most when I got back into her extra hot twat, that dick had her praying. As she talked to God, I was one laughing, dick serving guy.

Watching the ripples that ass of hers created, Jonsey pissed me off when she barked and cooed at the same time. "Don't nut in me, Casey. I'm not on birth control. I got things to do!"

Angry with her speaking in that manner, I pounded that sweet, wet spot of hers. Jonsey didn't know if she was coming or going, which had a smile on my face. One minute she was letting out loud whimpers of pleasure and the next she was begging me to pull out.

Caught Up In A D-Boy's Illest Love 2

Feeling my nut approaching, I aimed my dick towards the right corner of her twat. Pounding her tender spot as she tried to run from me, I snatched her ass by those brown hairs on her head, and put my mouth to her right ear before saying, "Since, you wanna act stupid and shit. I guess, I'll go the extra mile to trap yo' ass. Get ready to be in Jonzella's position."

As I shoved my throbbing dick as far as it could go inside of her, Jonsey whimpered, "Noooo, Cassseyy!"

Letting my little boys and girls go, I groaned in a satisfied tone, "Oh, yesss, Jonseyy! Now, it's time for us to go to bed. I did my job."

***

When I woke up, it was ten-thirty in the morning. Rolling over, I stared Jonsey in the face as she lightly snored. With a content smile on my face, I gently rubbed my sleeping lady's smooth face. After planting a kiss on her lips, I quietly slid out of the bed.

Strolling into the master bathroom, I drained the monster followed by taking care of my hygiene. Thirty minutes later, I was in the kitchen bobbing my head as I prepared a nice brunch meal.

Ding. Dong.

With a smirk on my face and a heavy sigh, I ambled towards the door. I wasn't in the mood for company. All I wanted to do was feed Jonsey and get back in between her stubborn legs. Opening the door, I glared at a stern faced Totta.

"What's wrong, nigga?" I voiced as I stepped to the side, letting him in.

"She won't talk to me," he angrily replied.

Closing the door, I said, "Did you pull up?"

Swiftly turning around to face me, that fool hollered, "Nigga, I don' pulled up. I don' tried to climb through her window. All that shit."

Trying not to laugh at him, I simply stared while shaking my head.

Continuing, Totta said, "Mane, I'm at my wit's end with Jonzella. I don't know how much longer I can take without talking to her. February 2 is too damn long, woe."

Soon as I opened my mouth, my doorbell chimed. Hearing my mother's, grandmother's, and father's voice made me say shit underneath my breath. Opening the door, they happily spoke.

"What a wonderful surprise," I voiced sarcastically as they waltzed into my home.

Everyone spoke to Totta, followed by hugging him. Totta and my father began strolling to the kitchen, chatting; as the women asked me a thousand questions.

"I'm in the process of cooking brunch for a special friend. Can y'all come back later?" I inquired soon as I stepped over the threshold of the kitchen.

With a smirk on his face, Totta replied, "I ain't going nowhere, mane. I ain't ate since seven o'clock last night. You ain't finna throw me to the side 'cause your queen in check."

"I guess you heard that," my grandmother chuckled as she gave Totta a high-five.

Rolling my eyes and resuming to my cooking duties, I had to inhale and exhale several times. I didn't want to blow on them, but I sure as hell was going to let them know they weren't welcome at the time.

As my family chatted lightly, they occasionally asked me questions, which I answered quickly. While I sautéed white onions and bell peppers, Jonsey called out for me.

"I'm in the kitchen, babe," I hollered with a smile on my face.

"Look at this ancient black nigga here, cheesing and stuff," Totta spat in a joking manner.

Already tired of his ass, I shook my head before hollering, "Jonsey, please call Jonzella and tell her to answer Totta's call. I'm tired of him whining to me."

That comment caused my family to laugh. The back and forth comments between Totta and I didn't stop until Jonsey waltzed into the kitchen, wearing one of my T-shirts and her jeans.

"Hello, everyone," she sweetly stated shyly.

Chuckling, I said, "Everyone, this is my lady, Jonsey. Jonsey, you've seen me with these two ladies before. However, I'll properly introduce y'all."

After I finished introducing Jonsey to my parents and grandmother, the damn doorbell chimed followed by, "Dank, I know you in there. Open the door."

"Ooouu, let me go and pop me some popcorn!" Totta shouted as he got up from the bar stool, aiming for my snack cabinet.

"Is that that crazy looking girl, Diamond?" my grandmother asked as I peeled away from the stove.

"Yeah," I replied dryly before strolling towards the door.

"Totta, will you take me home? I don't have time for drama," I heard Jonsey say in an agitated tone.

Before my partner could open his mouth, I loudly announced, "You ain't going nowhere. It ain't Totta's job to get you home ... it's mine."

"Oh, my. He so damn bossy." My messy grandmother chuckled, followed by her saying, "Come have a seat baby. Ain't nobody going to put their hands on you."

Ding. Dong. Ding. Dong. Ding. Dong.

"Stop playing on my doorbell like that, Diamond!" I yelled at the same time my grandmother left the kitchen table.

Sighing heavily as I opened the door, Diamond shoved her way inside of my home. With her hands on her hips, she said, "Um, your phone must be dead or something, Dank? Why haven't you responded to any of my messages?"

"Why are you here, Diamond?" I inquired, ignoring her questions.

"I want to know why are you playing these games with me, Dank."

Growing angry because I could imagine what Jonsey was thinking, I grabbed Diamond's arms—trying to lead her ass out of my home. I knew by me trying to put her out was going to lead into a full-fledged argument and altercation.

"Get your damn hands off me, Dank!" Diamond yelled.

"Then get the hell out of his home! You are not wanted here, hussy!" I heard Jonsey angrily shout as she came from the kitchen.

"Hussy!" Diamond shouted as she tried to break free from me.

Holding a tight grip on Diamond, Jonsey stood her ground and let Diamond have all her frustration and anger. The argument between the two started, and I swear a nigga caught a severe headache.

"Baby girl, you ain't nothing to this dope boy. Trust, I know. These niggas will tell y'all college bitches anything, and y'all dumbass fall for it. Dank, ain't gon' ever leave me alone. Know that. I am his true ridah...he knows!" Diamond shouted as she pulled away from me and stood firm while glaring at my lady.

"Diamond, I'm really starting to get pissed. You know what happens when I get that way right? I don't mind shooting anybody ... in case you forgot," I voiced sternly.

Quickly glancing at Jonsey, I saw hatred in Jonsey's eyes that I never thought she could possibly show. Seeing what I saw, I told her to go upstairs until I got the bitch out of my home. Ignoring what I said, Jonsey took off towards Diamond as Diamond started running towards Jonsey.

Knowing that I didn't want Jonsey to be fighting, I had to see Diamond get hers. Standing tall, I watched Diamond open her arms to possibly put Jonsey in a chokehold.

"Ooou, where is my phone?" Totta laughed as he rounded the corner in time to see Jonsey scoop Diamond in the air followed by slamming her on the ground.

"Milord, that lil' girl strong as hell," my mother voiced as my grandmother nodded her head.

With his phone in his hand, Totta was Jonsey's cheerleader. With a smile on my face, I watched the women throw blow after blow. Diamond's blows didn't faze Jonsey; however, I saw what Jonsey's blows were doing to Diamond.

"You played on my phone for the dick. You got weak for the dick. You getting that ass beat for the dick. Walking up in his home, talking plenty of shit for the dick. You got me mixed up with the other bitches for the dick. You making yourself relevant for the dick. You acting an ass about the dick...the same dick that belongs to me!" Jonsey angrily shouted as she placed her hands around Diamond's slender neck. I knew that Jonsey was applying pressure because Diamond's arms started flailing.

The entire time Jonsey was talking, my grandmother said, "My goodness, baby. She ain't doing all that for the dick is it? Casey, however you serving that thing in your pants, you need to stop it!"

Totta ignorant ass yelled, "Woe, I'm tryna be like you when I grow up!"

"Shut yo' ass up!" my grandmother spat while laughing before popping Totta upside his head.

"Son, break it up!" my father shouted. Ignoring him, I glared at my woman as she choked the bitch to sleep. Once Diamond was completely out, Jonsey was still choking her.

"That's enough, Jonsey. She's asleep. Back away," I told her as Totta and I strolled towards her.

Not hearing me, she continued to apply pressure. Dropping his phone on the floor, Totta snatched Jonsey off Diamond. Before I grabbed the broad's arm, I glared at Jonsey before saying, "Take her upstairs, Totta."

"A'ight," he voiced while nodding his head.

"Nawl, Totta, take me home," she nastily voiced while glaring at me.

"No! You go upstairs!" I yelled while giving her the same nasty look she gave me.

"You are not my daddy, dude!"

"I'm not about to argue with you, woman. Do as I say, and we will be good!" I sternly yelped back.

Evilly chuckling, she replied, "If I don't, what you gon' do? Put a bullet in me like you did my brothers?"

With a shocked facial expression, my parents and grandmother said, "What the fuck?"

"Jonsey, calm down, please," Totta's calm voice demanded.

I knew what that tone meant, and I hoped Jonsey saw in my eyes that it was time for her to shut the fuck up.

Sighing heavily, I said, "Totta, get Diamond out of here. Mom, Dad, and Grandma, I need some privacy with Jonsey."

"Okay," they replied in unison as they glared at Jonsey with worried eyes.

"Why do they have to leave? Wait a minute, why in the fuck am I still here? I gave you what you wanted. That was the deal. We sleep together, and then I go home. I overstayed my lil' welcome. Now, it's time for me to get on about my business," she voiced angrily before changing her tone. "Don't come behind me, and all of us will be good."

With a blank look upon my face, Jonsey trotted upstairs. Totta glared in my face and said, "Fix that shit, woe."

Stunned at the turn of events, I didn't know what to say or do. Granted that the ladies could get us jammed up, I was stuck in the same position. I could barely respond to Totta. He had to repeat his statement again. Out the corner of my eyes, I saw my parents and grandmother looking at me with a bewildered facial expression.

Shaking my head, all I could say, "Woe, the only way I know how to do that is to leave her alone."

Chapter 15
Jonzella

My morning was going okay until Totta and I strolled into Dr. Nyckerson's semi-packed, lovely decorated floral office and saw the ugly smirk on Erica and her friend's faces. With a pleasant smile on my face, I shook my head, followed by chuckling. If I was present for a routine check-up, I would've rescheduled just to avoid the bullshit; however, my little seed had to come first. After signing in, the mumbling of the broad and her entourage made Totta speak up, extremely loud with his ghetto ass.

"Erica and the oh so ugly crew, I'mma fa da need y'all to chill out. Please don't make me shut this place down. I'm trying to act right in Corporate America," he hissed as unwrapped his arms from around my waist while he glared into each of their faces.

Trying not to laugh at him, I held a smile on my face. With my eyes planted on the odd crew, Totta asked me, "You and my seed good, my queen?"

"*We* surely are," I responded calmly as I planted my eyes on the man that captured my heart and soul.

"Ugh, folks know they be doing the most for no reason," Erica sighed as the tone of jealousy was through her statement.

Being petty, I leaned over to Totta and put my head on his shoulder. Inhaling his scent, I had the sudden urge to stick my tongue in his mouth. As if he had read my mind, Totta lifted my face to his, followed by parting my glossy lips with his thick, minty tongue. Reciprocating the kiss, I forgot that we were in the doctor's office until a lady stated, "Those pregnancy hormones will do that to you."

Breaking the kiss with while blushing, I had a cheesy smile on my face. Making polite conversation with the woman, I felt better about becoming a mom. Ten minutes of us talking, the petite, young woman was called to the back. Glancing at my child's father as he glared at me, I eyed him in a naughty way. He had his grown man attire on, and I was a sucker for him when he wore any color of collared shirt, Sperry's, and khaki or white jeans.

"Why you staring at me like that, queen?" Totta voiced as he licked his lips while placing his left hand into my right hand.

"No reason," I lied with a slight smile on my face.

"Hmm, hmm. You gon' learn to stop lying to me," he voiced in a stern tone.

Ring. Ring. Ring.

"Ain't nobody lying to you," I lied as I quickly silenced my phone from Renee's call as I heard the nurse calling Erica's name.

With an ugly facial expression, I wondered what in the hell did she want, and how did she get my number. Seeing how I reacted to my phone, that baby daddy of mine had something to say, and he didn't sugarcoat shit.

"Who called your damn phone?" he hissed as he turned his entire to the left, facing me.

"Nobody," I replied honestly as glared into his brown eyes.

"Make me fuck you up, Jonzella," he voiced at the same time the sweet voiced nurse called my name.

Standing up, I looked at him and said, "You still on thin ice, dude...don't get it twisted."

On the verge of saying something, I cut it short by saying, "Let's go make sure that *we* are healthy."

Hopping up from the seat with a grim look on his face, he had his lips pressed tightly together as I slowly turned away from him.

Sashaying towards the lightly freckled faced woman with a smile on my face, I politely said, "Good morning."

After we said our pleasantries, we strolled towards the weight machine. Upon stepping onto the scale, I felt a strong wave of nausea consume my body. Holding my head back, I performed breathing exercises. Shortly after, the nausea disappeared. Seeing that I weighed one-hundred and forty-five pounds, I stepped off the scale.

Following behind the nurse, Totta said in a deep voice, "My queen getting thick."

Smiling, I replied, "Hush up."

Caught Up In A D-Boy's Illest Love 2

After spending ten minutes in the nurse's station, we were placed in examination room number four. Upon her informing us that the doctor would be in shortly, we said okay. Once the door was closed, Totta glared at me in a loving way. On the brinks of wanting to be nasty with him, I had to quickly remind myself that we were just going to co-parent and not participate in anything further.

"You are so beautiful, you know that?" he voiced as he interrupted my thoughts.

"Yes," I voiced in a low tone while biting down on my bottom lip.

Growling, he said, "Please stop doing that, queen. I'm in a mood to do something strange to you in this room."

Knock. Knock.

Saved by the knocks, I quickly thought before stating, "Come in," as I glanced at the door.

With a bright smile on her face, my gynecologist strolled in passing out 'hellos' and 'how are you's'. After she shook our hands, we got down to business. General questions, routine pregnancy check, followed by my physician telling me how far along I should be based off my period. With a due date in mind, she quickly told us that she was going to schedule me for an ultrasound the following week.

Soon as we exited the reception office with my next appointment and prenatal prescription, Totta grabbed my hand while looking in my eyes, "I'm going to do right by you and our baby. You do know that, right?"

Not wanting to put myself or him in a sour mood, I simply nodded my head.

"Look, I know I did some fu—" he began to say before a loud mouth Erica began yelling.

"While you are playing daddy to hers, make sure you are ready to be a daddy to mine!"

Dropping my hand, Totta turned around and laughed hysterically before saying, "Bitch, you crazy as hell. You honestly, think I will allow you to see nine months? There are too many stairs, concrete, and way too many cars I can flip over my whip to see you full-term. Now with that being said, go visit the abortion place on South Perry Street."

"You ain't making her have one, so I am not having one either," she spat with her hands on her hips.

"Bitch, you gon' do what I say willingly, or your pathetic life will be useless once I have you sterile for life!"

"All those threats you are making are useless to me … especially when I know what you and Dank did to those two dudes. Don't fuck with me, Joshua Nixon," she spoke clearly in confidence.

My God, I thought while standing against the back of my car.

The wind was knocked out of me as I completely understood she was implying and what really took place between them. In order for her to know his dirty deeds, they must've been pillow talking; something he never did with me. Feeling angry with myself more so than Totta, I politely walked behind him. Before I knew it, I slapped the hell out of him. Thrown off by my actions, Totta caught himself before he hit me.

"Jonzella, what did I tell you about keeping your hands to yourself?" he growled loudly with a mean facial expression.

"Fuck you and your dirty dick. I so don't want anything to do with you. There will be a middle person in this situationship we have created!" I yelled angrily while Erica was laughing and talking shit with her minions.

"Jonzella, get the fuck out of my face with that bullshit you talking. I already gotta deal with that bitch over there—" he stated before Erica cut him off.

"I ain't no bitch, dude. I surely wasn't a bitch when you were digging off in me. I was queen and baby then. Don't be fronting, my nigga," she yelped as she waltzed closer to us.

Shaking my head, I retrieved my keys. With them in my hand, I ran to my car. I wasn't going to be a part of the freak show Totta created. Starting the engine, I reversed my car as he was trying to get me to stop the car. Zooming away, the tears rolled down my face. I couldn't be mad at anyone but myself. I knew what I was dealing with when I began messing around with him; however, the mentioning of what he did to my brothers was the absolute no-no.

Ring. Ring. Ring.

Looking at the screen on my phone, I shook my head while ignoring the call. I was too distraught to talk to Renee. I didn't want to hear her lies or broken promises. I was simply done giving her a second of my time. There was nothing that she could say that would change the way I viewed her.

Soon as my phone stopped ringing, it started again. This time it was Totta calling. Quickly ignoring his call, I threw my phone on the passenger's seat. In need of having my prescription filled, I decided that I would visit Walmart on Atlanta Highway. In four minutes, I pulled into the busy parking lot. Seeing that there wasn't a close parking spot, I parked at the far end. Hustling out of my car, I ambled towards the front door.

In a world of my own, I didn't hear Totta calling my name until an older gentleman said, "My dear, a man is trying to get your attention."

Turning around, I growled as I replied, "That's a nobody but thank you for informing me."

Strolling about my business, I was in for a treat upon staring Renee Johnson in the face. Coming to a complete stand still, I clenched and unclenched my fists as I tried to remain calm. Trying to get my feet to move, they were glued to the very place I stopped. Seeing her waltz over to me pissed me off even more. Hearing Totta's voice behind me caused me to spaz out in my mind.

"I called you," Renee's smooth voice stated as she held out her arms.

With a stank facial expression, I glared at the woman. If she thought I was going to hug her, she was a great fool.

"Did you hear me, Jonzella...I said I called you," she repeated herself as Totta inquired who the woman was. I didn't say a word, but Renee did.

"I'm her mother."

"Umph, you must be Renee," he spat dryly.

"I am, and you are?" she asked with her hands on her petite hips.

"Mr. Not the One to Fuck With," my foolish ass child's father replied with bass in his voice.

The old Renee was in full force as she laughed before speaking, "Little boy, I will fuck your world up. Don't think–"

With his hand in his pocket, Totta stepped in Renee's face and glared before speaking, "Lady, don't think for a second that I don't know who you are and what you've put my queen through. Don't think for a second that I won't shoot your ass right here in these folk's store. The best thing you can do is walk away. I kill people for fun...especially when it threatens the life of my unborn child. Do...not...fuck...with...what's...mine."

Renee's eyes were bigger than mine once Totta was done talking to her. All I could do was stand there and look crazy. With a sea of people talking and walking around us, there was an eerie silence. Before I gathered the nerves to walk away, I asked Renee one question.

"Who is my real father?"

"I highly believe you already know the answer to that question," she stated smartly before plastering a smirk on her face.

"Bitch, you are pathetic," Totta spat at the same time he grabbed my hand. Snatching it away from him, I looked at him nastily before walking off.

The entire time I was in Walmart, Totta was on my heels, trying to get me to talk to him. I wasn't hearing anything that he said. I was more concerned with who my real father could be. Not sure whether to continue with my current thinking, I sighed heavily. I was one confused individual. Out of all my years of living, I never was worried about whom my father could be, and I wasn't sure why I cared now. I had a loving family. Knowing my real father shouldn't have made a big deal but it did.

"Jonzella, talk to me please," Totta begged as I sat on the bench, waiting on my prescription to be filled.

With my phone in my hand, I ignored him and called my dad. On the second ring, he answered the phone.

"How's my baby girl doing?"

"Not good, Dad. Are you able to talk?" I inquired as I felt the tears welling in my eyes.

"Yes, I can talk. What's wrong?" he questioned curiously.

"I just saw Renee."

Silence.

"Dad, did you hear me?"

"I did," he replied before exhaling heavily.

"Dad, please don't tell me that you told her what city I live in," I whined as I shook my head.

"I'm sorry, sweetie. I did. I think you should talk with her. I didn't say grow a relationship with, I said talk. Forgive her so that you can have some peace in your life," he voiced genuinely.

Not hearing any of the noise he was talking, I said, "I asked her who my real father was, and she told me that she highly believed that I already knew. So, Dad, are you my father?"

"Like I told you when you were here, either I'm your real father or the dude she was dating at the time. I never asked for a DNA, and I don't need one now, Jonzella. Why are you hell bent on wanting to know, now?"

Shrugging my shoulders as if he could see me, I didn't respond.

"Answer me, Jonzella," my father stated sternly.

"I don't know…I guess I've just been thinking heavily on it since Kyvin was so nasty at the hospital."

"Whether you have my blood or not, I don't care. I still love you. Truth be told, I would be hurt to know if you weren't mine. So, I guess that's why I never stressed on the issue. In my mind, you are my blood, and it's going to stay that way. Now, off that subject. How was the doctor's appointment?"

With a smirk on my face, I replied, "Okay. The baby is supposedly due around September 17th. I'm having an ultrasound done on my next visit."

"Good, good. Take care of yourself and don't let anything stress you out, okay?"

"Okay. I love you." My voice broke by the time I said love. Rubbing my back, Totta kissed me on my cheek as my daddy said that he loved me too, followed by him saying that he would talk to me later.

Ending the call, my name was called. Totta told me that he would retrieve my medicine. Soon as he paid for it, a woman and two girls called his name while strolling towards him. Sighing heavily, I hopped up, snatched my medicine out of his hand, and sped passed them. I was not in the mood for another group of bitches wanting to get at me because of him.

"Jonzella, mane, where are you going? Can you please cut out the attitude?" he barked.

"I'm not about to argue with you or any other female over you. So, fuck off!" I yelled as I held up my middle finger.

"Ugh!" he voiced loudly before saying, "Mane, come back here and meet my mom and sisters."

Coming to a complete stop, I dropped my head. Feeling like a true asshole, I was embarrassed for my behavior. Now, I had to deal with the thoughts of what his siblings and mother thought of me. Slowly turning around, I tried to make eye contact with them; however, my feelings of how I just behaved had me on edge. Soon as I approached them, I extended my hand before politely saying, "I'm sorry that you had to witness me in that attitude. I'm Jonzella."

Shaking my hand, each of them said that it was okay followed by telling me their names.

"Totta, she's very beautiful," his mother stated as his sisters agreed.

"I got taste...y'all better act like it," he joked, which caused me to growl. Pinching myself hard, caused me to keep my mouth sealed.

"How did the doctor's appointment go? When is the baby due?" his mother piped as we slowly moved away from the pharmacy department.

Surprised that he told them about my pregnancy, I kept quiet and let him do all the talking.

"September 17th," he voiced happily.

"I'm assuming the bag you are holding are prenatal vitamins, Jonzella?" his sweet voiced mother stated.

"Yes, ma'am," I replied shyly.

"Did Totta tell you that I invited y'all over for dinner?" she inquired.

"No, ma'am," I replied while shaking my head.

"Don't shake your head, queen. I didn't get a chance to tell you because of the bull that happened," he voiced.

"Hmm, umm." I shot back with great attitude.

He was about to say something, but I nipped it in the bud.

"It was a pleasure meeting you, lovely ladies. I'm not feeling well. Maybe we can have lunch or dinner another time."

"No, ma'am. Tonight. We know what happened between you and my son. Trust, we grilled him out for his foolish antics, and yes, he did feel like an asshole by the time we were done talking to him. Don't let his foolish ways stop you from being a good woman and doing the right thing, Jonzella. You don't have to deal with my son, but you do have us...his mother and sisters, who are eager to love our new family member. So, tonight you will be at my home as we get to know each other, and that's the end of discussion. Okay?" his mother voiced with a pleasant smile on her face.

Nodding my head while looking at each of the ladies, I finally said, "Okay."

Before we had the chance to say goodbye, the ghetto hoodrat, Erica stormed over and said, "Hello, everyone. Since, Totta is introducing *her*. I guess I might as well introduce myself. I'm Erica.

Totta's other baby momma. I'm due October 10th. How are y'all on this lovely day?"

Chapter 16
Totta

Honestly, a brother didn't expect any more crazy shit to pop off since I left Jonzella's doctor's office. To my surprise, Erica stepped to my family and spat that nonsense. If the sheriff hadn't walked towards us, I would've shot the shit out of Erica. Instead of me showing my ass, it was Jonzella busting Erica's nose and lip, followed by kicking her in the stomach. I dragged Jonzella off the dusty foot broad.

As the sheriff tried talking to us, I kept moving along—with my queen in my arms. My mother and sisters conversed with the sheriff. I sure as hell didn't have a thing to say to him or anyone else. Placing Jonzella at her car, she didn't say a word to me as I tried to calm her. Getting in her car, she didn't attempt to look my way as she sped away.

Shaking my head, I exhaled before saying, "This is too much for one nigga to deal with."

Approaching my whip, my cell phone began to ring. Grabbing it out of my pocket, I noticed that my mother was calling. Quickly answering the phone, I said, "Hello."

"Get yo' black ass to my house now!" she screamed, angrily.

Knowing what type of mood she was in, all I could reply was, "Yes, ma'am."

"You make sure that Jonzella is at my house with you."

"She's pissed with me, but I'll try," I voiced as I unlocked the car doors.

"Don't try...do it!" she snapped before ending the call.

Fleeing Wal-Mart's parking lot, I tried to reach out to Jonzella. It was useless as I was being sent to voicemail. Seeing that calling her was useless, I decided to pull up at her home. Ignoring the speed limits and yellow lights, I had one thing on my mind and that was making things right between Jonzella and me. Not for the sake of our baby, but because I really loved that woman. Never had I been that crazy over a female before. Not one female that I dealt with made me want to leave the streets or cared less about serving a junkie. Truth be told, Jonzella was the reason why ToTo and Benut were dead. Trying to hang out and do something nice for her, led me to forget that I made previous sales.

My thoughts ceased the moment, I pulled into her driveway. Leaving the engine running, I hopped out and jogged to the front door. Knocking several times, I called her name. It took some time for her to answer the door, and all I could do was stare at her glossy, wet eyes. I badly wanted to wrap her in my arms, but fear of her struggling to get away from me ceased me doing so.

"What do you want, Totta?"

"Momma, wants you to come over with me, right now."

"No. I'm not feeling well," she replied, trying to close the door.

"Jonzella, my ass is on the line if I don't bring you with me. You don't know, but a nigga scared of his mother. So, please don't bring that heat towards me," I begged, telling her the truth.

Ring. Ring. Ring.

Pulling my phone out of my pocket, I slid my hand across the answer button followed by hitting the speaker button.

"Hello," I voiced lightly.

"Where yo' ass at?" my mother yelped.

"Trying to get Jonzella to come in the car with me."

"Well, I'm ten minutes away from my house. Y'all asses better be there by the time I get there. If not, you know what I'm going to do!"

"But, Momma, I can't make her come—" I began to say before my mother yelled, "I don't give no fucks. Not do what I say and see how bad I'mma whoop your ass."

Knowing damn well that she hung the phone up, I looked at Jonzella with pleading eyes before saying, "My queen, please come with me. I just got my ass whooped for eating her cookies. That woman is crazy. Can you please spare me another marathon of running up and down my mother's neighborhood? I'll do whatever you want."

Seeing a faint smile on her face, my lady nodded her head. Dipping to her room, she returned with her keys in her hand. Locking and closing the door behind, I quickly informed her that she was riding with me. Nodding her head, she waltzed towards the passenger's side of my whip.

Walking behind her, I said, "Don't you open that door. It's my job from here on out, understood?"

"Understood," she replied lowly.

The ten-minute ride to my mother's house was the longest trip ever. Jonzella didn't say anything no matter what I said to her. She simply nodded her head or had a smirk on her face. Exhaling sharply, I simply gave up—for the moment. I wasn't willing to let her out of my life.

Turning into my mother's yard, my heart was beating a mile a minute as I saw her standing on the porch with a stern look on her face. Hopping out of the car, I waltzed towards my passenger's door. Opening it, Jonzella slipped out without placing her eyes on me. It seemed as if a brother was walking on the green mile; it was a creepy silence amongst us. The moment we stepped on the porch, Jonzella told my mother that she had a lovely home and yard. Placing a smile on her face, my mother replied, "Thank you, darling. Come inside and welcome to my home."

With a pleasant smile on her face, Jonzella strolled inside with me right behind her. Sniffing heavily, I didn't smell any food cooking.

Quickly turning around to face my mother, I said, "Momma, you ain't started on dinner yet?"

"Nope. You got my pressure up so high; I can't focus in the kitchen right now. I sent your sisters to Panera Bread to get soup and sandwiches for lunch," she announced as she closed the screen door behind her.

Ushering Jonzella to the living room, we took a seat on the sofa. Moments later, my mother strolled in. With a stern facial expression, I knew that she was ready to go off on me. After she inhaled and exhaled several times, she finally spoke.

"Jonzella, I know you've had a hard time dealing with my son, and I honestly understand your frustration with him. What he said to you was unacceptable. I didn't raise him to neglect his responsibility. Whatever you choose to do regarding keeping him in y'all's baby's life, is your decision; however, don't make the wrong decision that could hurt the baby. If you don't want to talk or be around my son, then y'all need to talk it out and find a person that is willing to be involved in this situation. I'm willing to be the communicator for you two. His sisters are also. Okay?"

"Okay," Jonzella voiced as she gave my mother her full attention.

"Now, Totta, whatever she chooses to do, if it's not what you want to do, then you will have to suck it up. You brought shit on yourself. My advice to you is that you learn from your mistakes. Bringing babies into this world is an easy task, but it's hard once your child is born. Understanding, commitment, dedication, passion, and knowledge have to be met at every second of the day.

Your entire life will shift, and everything will be about the baby and not so much as about the parents."

"Do y'all understand what I'm saying?" my mother asked us.

"Yes," Jonzella and I replied in unison.

"Joshua Nixon, who is that heifer that said she was your second baby momma?"

"She lying," I stated, quickly.

"I didn't ask you that! I asked you who the fuck she is."

Before I could open my mouth to say something, Jonzella beat me to the punch. "A girl that goes to school with me. Her name is Erica Romans. We've bumped heads about your son before. Today, wasn't the first time.

Shaking her head, my mother said, "I told you 'bout those types of girls, boy. You can't stick your dick in everything raw. You ain't gon' be satisfied until that motherfucker fall off in your hands. All I know is that if you highly don't believe that baby is yours, you better get a DNA test."

"She ain't going to keep that seed," I blurted out. Realizing that I said that in front of the wrong woman, I wanted to bust myself in the face.

"And what the fuck does that mean?" my mother asked with an attitude.

"Nothing, Momma."

"Oh, yes it does. If it didn't, then you wouldn't have said it. So, please explain," she demanded with her hands on her hips.

Sighing heavily and avoiding eye contact, I spat, "If she survived the way Jonzella kicked her in the stomach, then she will surely come face to face with several stairs and/or the abortion clinic."

Throwing her head back, my mother sighed before saying, "Lord, why must my son be so darn crazy. Why does he feel that violence is always the way to do things?"

Before I had time to answer her questions as if I was God, my cell phone began to chime. Retrieving it from my pocket, I saw Danzo's name on the screen.

Answering the phone, I said, "Speak to me."

"Woe, you need to get that ass to my crib, ASAP," he rapidly voiced in the phone.

On alert mode, I said, "Why?"

"A broad out here talking mad shit about you. I had to snatch that bitch in my crib. She talking too much for me. She can land us in prison, yo," he voiced in an agitated tone.

"I'm on the way," I responded angrily at the same time my mother stated, "You ain't going no damn where, boy."

Hanging up the phone, I looked at Momma and replied, "If I don't leave now, that dusty bitch, Erica, will have me in prison for life. I gots to go."

With a smirk on her face, Jonzella shook her head. Kissing her forehead while rubbing her stomach, I quickly said, "I love you, and I'll be back soon as I can."

As I waltzed passed my mother, in a low tone, she asked, "What are you going to do to her?"

Coming to a complete stop, I slowly turned around and glared into my mother's beautiful eyes before saying, "I'm probably going to place my gun to her head, followed by squeezing the trigger."

"Totta, Totta, Totta, my son, don't do it. Wait for one of your sisters to go with you. Have them whoop the bitch," Momma said calmly.

"That ain't good enough," I replied before darting towards the door.

The moment I hopped in my whip, I threw on the hazard lights. It was going to take me fifteen minutes to pull up at Danzo's crib. With the thoughts of having a peace of mind, murdering Erica, being a daddy, and wanting to marry Jonzella on my mind, I knew I had to do the safest, dirty deed to the bitch, Erica.

Pulling out my phone, I rang Danzo's line. On the fourth ring, he answered.

"Woe, do you have some Visine? My eyes red as fuck," I replied, hoping he was able to catch on to what I was saying.

Chuckling, he replied, "Nigga, you know I keep that shit handy. I got a big ass bottle of it. I'll go ahead and pull it out for you."

"A'ight. I'll be there in a few."

"Bet. What the jealous bitch doing?"

"Sitting on the sofa, looking dumb as hell. I think I got the little bitch scared," he snickered.

"You must've done some nasty shit to her?" I inquired with a sneaky look on my face.

"I did!"

"My nigga."

Ending the call, I was glad that he was giving that bitch something to do with her mouth. I bet she wished she would've left me the fuck alone. I was crazy as hell, and every nigga around me was equally throwed off.

Eager to do a careless crime, I ran several red lights. After I ran the last light, I was turning into Danzo's street. It was a crowd of folks outside, and I hope that they didn't hear anything that Erica had to say. Unlike what we did to Benut and ToTo's ass, I was going to take the bitch to her house. Parking my car on the curb, I shut off the engine and hopped out. Not verbally speaking to anyone, I threw up the deuces. Strolling towards the front door, I started beating on the door in a silly manner. That was the code for Danzo to know it was me. Shortly after, he opened the door. We dapped each other up while politely chattering.

Soon as the door was closed, I looked at the nothing bitch and said, "You have no idea of the treat I'm going to give you."

Caught Up In A D-Boy's Illest Love 2

Not caring if she was going to respond, I strolled to the kitchen and grabbed a cup. Filling the red plastic cup with Patron, I asked Danzo, "Where the Visine at?"

"In the bathroom, woe," he stated as he waltzed in the kitchen.

With the cup in my hand, I ambled towards his bathroom. Within three seconds, I had the large bottle of eye drops in my hand. Leaving the poorly cleaned area, I happily whistled. Upon sitting next to her, Danzo stood in front with his gun drawn. As I poured the Visine in the drink, I talked to her calmly.

"All you had to do was leave me alone. You was just a fuck. Yeah, I fucked up and slipped my dick in you raw. However, you did the most when you simply didn't listen to me. Now, I'm tired of talking. You will drink all of this drink, followed by snorting three lines of crystal meth."

Tears flowing down her dirty face, she wept while saying, "I'm sorry, Totta. I love you. It's not fair how you are treating me for a bitch that isn't proud to have you on her arms. Why must you treat me like this? I've been down with you for quite some time. I've done everything that you've asked."

Ignoring everything she said, I extended the cup to her followed by saying, "Drink...all of it."

Hesitating, she stared at me until Danzo put the gun to her head. With shaky hands, Erica placed the cup to her lips and downed the concoction. Soon as she dropped the cup on the floor, I reached in my pocket and pulled out a small bag filled with my potent dope. Untying the bag, I handed it to her and commanded, "Sniff...all of it."

Crying, she did as I asked of her. Slumping back on the sofa, I hopped off the sofa all the while shaking my head. Waltzing into the kitchen, I grabbed a dish towel. Cleaning the areas that I touched in the kitchen, I ran to the bathroom and cleaned what I touched, and finally, I cleaned the areas in the front room that I touched and the spillage of the small contents in the plastic cup. Seeing Erica high as hell, I stuffed the rag in the plastic cup before grabbing it and her. With her legs loosely wrapped around me, I told Danzo that I would holler at him later.

"A'ight, woe," he voiced as he closed the door behind me.

Not worried about the crowd, I talked to Erica lovingly as if she was my woman. I did it all for show. Securing her in the front seat, I ambled towards the driver's side. Once inside of the car, I laughed. Pulling away from the curb, I was still in tears at the dumb bitch slumped over in the seat. She couldn't move or say shit as she looked at me. Zooming towards Hope Hull, I couldn't wait until I got the bitch out of my car. If someone would've told me months ago that I was going to do some dirty shit like this to Erica, I would've never asked for her number.

"The day I met you, Erica, I knew you was going to be on my team for a while. You was down for the street life. I knew you were going to be my ridah. You had a nigga's back like no other broad has had it. See, you fucked up a good thing when you came for Jonzella. That was a no-no. Your only job with me was to be the second bitch ... not the main. You didn't have the qualifications to be the main bitch. Then you want to run your mouth on a serious tip. Do you honestly think that I was going to let you go? Hell nawl, bitch, I got too many people that lives depend on me," I told the lethargic broad.

As I continued to talk to the unresponsive broad, I arrived at my destination. Pulling into a heavily wooded area, I smoked two blunts before discarding of the dumb chick's body. Truth be told, I didn't know the outcome of what would happen to her; however, I was confident that something was going to happen to her. Either a stray animal would feast on the bitch, the drugs were going to take a hold of her, or someone was going to find her alive and try to get her help; regardless of what happened to her, she was going to know that I wasn't to be fucked with.

"If you survive this, bitch you better never seek me or I will kill your entire family, even the fucking babies. Think I'm playing, try me," I voiced lowly before throwing her body into the tall, thick, green bushes.

Leaving the same way that I came in, I fled the area. Wanting to dial Jonzella's number, I refrained from doing so. I didn't want to take any chances of having my cell phone number jumping off any towers, in case the police found the bitch's body. Twenty-five minutes later, I was pulling into my mother's driveway. I saw the ladies sitting on the porch chatting and laughing. Stepping out of my car, everyone was silent.

Approaching the porch, my mother said one word, "Shower."

Nodding my head, I did as she asked of me. Upon entering the bathroom, a soft knock sounded off.

Knowing who it was, I said, "Come in."

As the door opened, I stripped out of my clothes and shoes. Jonzella waltzed in with a black plastic bag. With gloves on her hands, she discarded my shoes, socks, pants, boxers, and my two shirts in the bag. Sighing heavily as she tied the bag, she placed her brown eyes on me. Biting down on my bottom lip, I had so much that I wanted to say, yet I didn't. The look I gave her said a thousand things. I wanted to smile, but I couldn't. If I thought that Erica was the true rider, I was dead ass wrong. Here was the woman that swore I killed her brothers, putting my clothes in a bag—that spoke volumes to me.

"I don't condone in what you have done to my brothers and to that bitch. However, my child will not be without his daddy," she softly stated before placing her hand on the doorknob.

"I wanted to kill your brothers. I sought after them. However, before I made that call to knock them off the map, someone else did that job. I promise you I didn't kill them. I saw them get shot,

but it wasn't me that made that call, queen. If I did, I would own it,"
I told her calmly.

"I got the illest love for my unborn, so don't get shit twisted,
Joshua Nixon," she stated with a little bass in her voice before
continuing. "You said that you'll do whatever I want you to, right?"

Nodding my head, I said, "Hell yes."

"Good. Now, take a shower so that we can lie down. I'm sleepy,"
she commanded before walking out of the bathroom.

Once the door was closed, my heart was somewhat at peace.
However, I knew that Jonzella had something up her sleeves. What
it was? I truly didn't know, but I bet it had something to do with
her biological mother. Turning on the water knobs, I waited a
while before stepping into the shower. As I placed my left foot in
the tub, another set of soft knocks sounded off. Jonzella didn't give
me time to say come in before she waltzed her ass in, followed by
locking the door. I watched her peel off her clothes. My eyes were
locked in on her growing breasts. Instantly, my mouth salivated at
the same time my dick got hard.

Walking towards me, Jonzella cooed, "You need to feed our seed,
don't you think?"

Nodding my head, I replied, "Yes, I do, but dang we at my momma
crib. We gotta wait until we leave."

"Nawl, now," she barked with an attitude as she placed two of my
fingers inside of her.

The wetness and the soft coos that left her mouth caused me to scoop her ass up. Sliding my dick inside of Jonzella caused us to passionately whimper in unison.

"You want some of this illest loving, my queen?"

"I doooo," she moaned as she began to rotate her hips.

"Well, I guess I have no choice but to give it to you," I groaned as I began stroking her pussy, rapidly.

Chapter 17
Jonsey

After I came home from school, I was a mess. I didn't want to do anything other than lay on my bed and sulk in misery. Jonzella wasn't home, so I had no one to talk too. I knew that she was out with Totta, so I decided to give them space so that they could work out their problems. I was in dire need of hearing from Casey, but I knew that wasn't the best route—given how I showed my ass Monday night. I didn't feel any shame of how I acted or what I said.

Since I left Casey's home, I didn't know what to do about our relationship. I didn't know how to properly think about anything that was going on with me. Whenever I felt the urge to contact him, I would feel guilty. When I was on the brinks of calling him, I felt guilty. I was confused as hell, and I didn't like it one bit. All I knew was that I had to find solace. Headaches were coming to me left and right, and I was tired of swallowing pain pills.

Ring. Ring. Ring.

Looking down at my phone, I saw that my father was calling. Quickly answering the phone, I said, "Hello."

When he didn't respond, I said hello two more times until I realized that he was talking to someone else. A particular someone that almost destroyed me, my ex-thug of a boyfriend, Damente

Wilks. Extremely eager to know what they had going on, I grew quiet and listened to their conversation.

"You did a great job," my father said in a professional timbre.

"Thank you," Demante responded as I assumed they shook hands.

"I need you to hand me the phones and laptops that you used to communicate with me," my father commanded, sternly.

"Not without the payment that you owe me. A deal is a deal. I honored my end … now it's time for you to honor yours," my ex spoke confidently.

What in the hell have they been doing? I thought as my dad sighed before responding, "The insurance company has not paid us yet."

With bucked eyes, I sat up in the bed. I was eager to know what in the hell was going on, and I prayed that my father didn't have my brothers killed and had Demante do it! Needing to know more, I remained quiet. I barely breathed in fear that my father would realize that I was on the phone.

Demante angrily spat, "You didn't say anything about paying me with insurance money for killing your sons. If I had of known that, I would've asked for the deposit up front."

Gasping loudly, I covered my mouth. Shaking my head repeatedly, I wanted to scream no; yet, I knew that wasn't in my best interest. Wishing that Jonzella was home to hear the conversation, I couldn't wait until I was able to inform her of what

I learned. I knew the moment I got off the phone, I had to find Casey and apologize to him.

"You will get your money as soon as I am paid, Demante."

"Well, when I get the payments...you will get the devices. Until, then don't call me unless you have my $3,000," my ex quickly spat.

Wow, Dad murdered his sons for $3,000. What in the hell is wrong with him? I wonder was Mother in on the dirty acts? I questioned myself as my father sighed sharply before speaking.

"What item on this property of mine do you want?"

"Nothing. I want what you owe me!" Demante shouted.

Where is Mom? I thought after hearing Demante yell what he wanted.

"I'll call you the moment the insurance company sends me the money," my father stated in a defeated timbre.

"Good," Demante voiced before asking, "Where's Jonsey's fine ass at?"

"Don't fuck with me, boy!"

Chuckling, my ex replied, "You don't have to tell me...I know she's in Montgomery, Alabama. I also know exactly where she lives. Your stupid ass sons led me to her and Jonzella's home. If you don't have my money within fourteen days, I guess I will have to pay her pussy a visit. You know she loved it when I dicked her down. After all, I was the first to get that pussy...oops, you already know that since you was the reason I went after her in the first place...OG Brown."

With tears streaming down my face, I had to know what was really going on and had been going on. I waited for my father to respond to Demante, but it never happened. The room had an eerie silence before the line went dead. Looking down at my phone to see what happened, it informed me that the call ended. In panic mode, I didn't know what to do since I heard some shit that I wasn't supposed to have heard—that I was sure off. Taking some time to get my thoughts together, I didn't know how I should act if my father called my phone. One thing I knew for certain was that I couldn't trust him. Hell, I was afraid of being around him. If he had Kenny and Kevin murdered, who's to say that he won't have the same thing done to the remainder of his children.

Five minutes passed before I dialed Casey's number. He didn't answer; thus, I called Jonzella's phone. When she didn't answer, I grabbed my keys, slipped on my shoes, and fled our home. In search of Casey, I turned down his grandmother's street. Seeing his car making a right turn at the stop sign, I sped behind him. Making the same turn that he did, I mashed the gas pedal all the while honking my horn. I knew without a doubt that he saw me behind him, yet he continued driving, until he approached another stop sign. Seeing that the traffic was heavy on Ann Street, in both directions, I placed my gearshift in park, hopped out, and ran like hell to the driver's side of his car.

I thought that upon seeing me that he would roll down the windows, instead he kept those fuckers up. Not in the mood for his bullshit, I banged on his window until my fist hurt. Seconds later, the window came down and an angry, Casey spat, "What?"

"We need to talk right now. Can we, please?" I begged.

"Nawl, Ms. Lady, we are good. I'm done with the circus game and you," he spat before pulling off.

Standing in the middle of the road like a fool, I cried as I watched him zoom away. Not the one to give up, I hopped in my vehicle and aimed for his home. Not sure if he was going there or not, I knew that whenever he pulled into his yard I was going to be right there.

***

I was awakened by a woman giggling. Looking crazy as I zoned in on where I was at, I realized that I was still sitting in my car in Casey's front yard. Taking a quick glance at the clock on my dashboard, it showed that it was three a.m. Seeing Casey entering his home as he ushered a woman inside made me angry as hell. Hopping out of my car, I ran to his door. I was angry as hell. He didn't have to do me the way that he was. How could he after saying that he cared for me?

Bam. Bam. Bam.

I didn't want to seem as if I was like that chick Diamond, but I had to get his attention. Not answering the first three knocks on the door, caused me to bam on his door again. A few seconds later, Casey was coming to the door with his shirt off and pants unzipped.

On the verge of crying, I stammered, "Why are you ignoring me?"

"After the scene you made, I don't want anything to do with you, Jonsey," he stated casually as the woman in the background cooed his name.

Seeing that I was on the bad end of the stick, I simply stated, "I'm sorry for what I said and how I behaved. I no longer believe that you and Totta harmed my brothers. Umm, have a nice life."

After I spoke to him, I ran to my car. Tears were streaming down my face, the moment I heard him close and lock his door. I just knew that he was going to tell the woman to leave and for me to come in. My heart was broken, my soul was torn, and my ego was destroyed. I felt like a complete fool. I didn't know how to control my emotions, so I just let the tears and my wails consume me.

Driving home, I hated that I loved him so. I hated that I gave him a chance. I hated that my brothers had to run across them, and I certainly hated that I wanted to turn around and run my entire car inside of Casey's home! Soon as I pulled in my driveway, I tried to reach out to Jonzella one more time. This time she answered the phone.

"Hello," she said sleepily.

"They aren't guilty...father is. I heard the entire conversation between him and Demante," I quickly rushed in the phone.

"Whoa, whoa, slow down, Jonsey. Now, calmly tell me what you just said ... you know what, fuck that; this type of conversation is not for the phone. I'm on my way home," she voiced before telling Totta that she needed to go home.

As she struggled to wake him up, Jonzella told me that she would be home the moment Totta woke up. With the call ended, I sat on the sofa Indian style, staring at the black TV screen. I badly wanted to call Casey, but I refrained from doing so. I had a thousand questions going on inside of my head, and I couldn't answer one of them. As my mind traveled to the conversation amongst my father and Demante, I found myself growing angry. Cursing and throwing the pillows off the sofa, I wanted them to hurt badly. I was disgusted at what they had done. Not only did they fuck up my relationship, they fucked up my mental.

"What in the hell is going on?" Jonzella spat the moment her and Totta stepped through the door.

With tears streaming down my face, I told them what I learned. Jonzella would've collapsed on the ground, if it wasn't for Totta catching her. By the time I was done talking, they stared at me as I glared at them. Sometime passed before Jonzella spoke, and when she did, I didn't know what to say.

"What are we going to do?"

"I don't know," I replied honestly.

Exhaling heavily, Totta announced, "All I can tell y'all to do is either act like you don't know shit, or to confront your father on it. Now, with that being said...if that nigga 'tempts to act like he wanna harm y'all, I'm a certified killer, and I will blow his fucking head off."

Jonzella didn't flinch or say anything to Totta's remark as well as I didn't. Looking down at the ground, Totta stated casually, "Jonsey, did you tell Casey what you told us?"

Hearing my love's name, I started crying.

"Whoa, what happened?" Totta voiced.

"I told him that I highly believed that you and him didn't hurt my brothers. He isn't fucking with me anymore. He dealing with someone else now. I saw them together at his house, that's when I told him," I cried as I refused to look at either of them.

"Why in the hell is he fucking with someone else? I thought y'all were o—" Jonzella began to say before Totta replied, "Jonzella, what I told you about that. Don't get in their business."

Not liking what Totta had to say, I placed my eyes on him before snapping. "Yet, it was cool for you to tell him to handle me when I said what I had to say at his house Monday night!"

"Okay, Totta, get to my room now," Jonzella voiced calmly as she slid in front of me.

Before he left, Totta announced, "What you said was unacceptable especially with the amount of people in his home. You could've gotten us thrown in prison for life with your comment. That's why I told him to handle you. You let your emotions get the best of you…that's why he isn't fucking with you and probably never will."

"Fuck you! If it wasn't for me telling Jonzella to do the right thing by the child she's carrying, you wouldn't be in her good graces!" I shouted.

"Jonsey, I know you are frustrated and pissed off, but you need to calm down. Don't dwell on anything that you learned from Daddy and what you did Monday. Please go and get some sleep. It's early in the morning. We will figure this shit out…together, but I have to get me some sleep. I'm off tomorrow. We can think on things later, okay?"

"Okay," I replied as we hugged, followed by kissing each other on the cheek.

As I watched my sister stroll to her room, I felt empty inside. The only thing I knew to do when I felt like that was to empty a bottle of liquor. Running to the kitchen cabinet, I pulled out the closest bottle—a sixteen-ounce, vodka Pinnacle bottle. Before I left the kitchen, I ensured that I drained the bottle followed by throwing it in the garbage can.

Caught Up In A D-Boy's Illest Love 2

Wobbling to my room, angry thoughts consumed me. Plopping on my bed, I was ready to act on those thoughts. My body relaxed, causing me to lay down and forget those thoughts. The images of Casey pleasing another woman zoomed in my head, causing me to cry and beat on my pillow until I fell asleep.

Chapter 18
Dank

Tuesday, February 14th

Normally, it wouldn't take me long to get over a female; however, the tricks I did to cease Jonsey from my mind wasn't working. No matter how many broads I dicked down or was around, they still didn't take that girl off my mind. Wanting to hear her voice, I would call her phone blocked. After the second day of calling private, Jonsey stopped answering the phone—she sent the calls instantly to voicemail. Then, I started stalking her Facebook page. Once I saw that she wasn't posting, I exited the social media website with a pout on my face.

Slumping further into my chair, my doorbell dinged. Ambling towards the door with a sad face, I wanted to sink into the ground.

Upon opening the door, Totta said, "Damn, dog, you look a hot ass mess. You gotta come out of that funk, dude. Either you call her or do what you need to do to get over her. Carrying on like this ain't gon' help you."

Ignoring him, I closed and locked my door. Waltzing back to sitting area, I plopped in my chair as Totta raided my 'fridge. Thinking on what he said, I knew that I had to make a decision and stick with it; however, I wasn't sure which one was the best for me.

Coming out of the kitchen, Totta said, "Let's hit up Club Freeze's V-Day bash."

"A'ight," I replied, not looking at him.

Silence overcame us as he reached for the remote control. Putting the TV on ESPN, I zoned out as the sportscasters started talking. Not in the mood for anything but smoking, I pulled out a fat sack of weed. Totta threw me several cigars, and I began busting them down. After stuffing the first six blunts with weed, I began on the last six. Once done, I handed Totta three blunts and we fired them up. As he smoked, he began talking; of course, I wasn't listening.

Three hours passed by before he left. Once he was gone, I started thinking about Jonsey. My mind didn't come off her until my phone started chiming. Seeing who was calling me, I answered the phone.

"What's good?" I piped nonchalantly.

"Can I come over?" the latest chick I was digging in asked.

"Yeah, Resheena, come over and bring your friend too," I voiced as I rubbed my growing man.

"Anything for you, Dank," she cooed before ending the call.

Jumping off the sofa, I aimed for the bathroom. Wanting to be fresh before the ladies arrived, I took a shower and brushed my teeth. I knew it was about to go down. I was going to have a fucking feast in every inch of my home—minus my bedroom. Ass, titties, pussy, and my dick was going to be swinging from ceiling fans as I tried to get Jonsey off my mind, for good! I had to become the ruthless, uncaring Casey to do that.

Forty-five minutes later, I was making them hoes do everything in the book, from eating each other out, to sucking my toes and shit. When it came down to fucking, they had me in awe of the tricks they performed on the D; however, they didn't make me feel like Jonsey did.

Nowhere near busting a nut, I hollered, "Y'all get the fuck out!"

Looking at me like I was crazy, I stated what I said but with more bass and authority in my voice. As they ran to the kitchen to retrieve their clothing, I was ushering their asses out of my home. Feeling like a complete asshole for thinking that I could fuck my way out of my feelings, I was one angry nigga. I was equally pissed at Jonsey; if her ass would've done right and shut the fuck up, then I would be one happy ass nigga.

"Don't call my line again!" I barked as they opened the car doors they were riding in.

"Gladly," the friend of Resheena's stated while Resheena shook her head with a disappointed facial expression.

Closing and locking my door, I began tearing that motherfucker up. Pictures were slung off the walls, the cushions were knocked off the sofas, DVD's were punched off the entertainment center, and holes were kicked in the walls, all the while I was cursing myself and Jonsey out for how I behaved. When I came too, I noticed the disaster I made in my home. I see I had sense not to fuck with my game system, those expensive ass TVs, and two glass tables.

Shaking my hanging head, I trotted to my bedroom. Flopping face down on the unmade bed, a nigga cried from frustration and confusion. Something I hadn't done in a long time!

***

Breezing through the club with two bottles of Hennessy and a Corona, I was on cloud nine. Itching to curse a bitch out, I was. Waiting on a nigga to come sideways, I was. Ready to bust my gun, I was. In the mood to tear up the club for no reason, I was! The sight of women didn't do anything but piss me off. There was only one woman that I wanted to see, but then again, I didn't need to see her. There was no telling what I was going to say or do to her.

"Stoner" by Young Thug blasted through the speakers, and naturally, I bobbed along to the beat. Sliding to the sitting area with The Savage Clique, I was surprised to see their Chief in attendance. Paying homage to X before any of the fellas, I strolled towards her and extended my hand. Taking her soft hands into mine, she pulled me close before saying in my ear, "You on a cloud none of us are on, eh?"

Chuckling, I nodded my head before saying, "Women problems."

"Ahh," she voiced quickly before saying, "Is she worth the pain you are going through?"

"I'm trying to figure that one out," I told her truthfully.

"Well, if you aren't yourself because of her...then you need to make things right for the better," she replied before telling me that love is the best thing when you have it with the right person.

Nodding my head as I looked in her eyes, I wondered how in the hell would she know, if she was incapable of loving anyone other than her loyal goons. Knowing not to ask, I ambled towards Totta as "Trap House" by Gucci Mane played. Drunk and high as hell, I rapped the song as I did my dance of jigging and moving my body along with the beat, in a manly way. A chick jumped in front of me, dancing and rapping, I politely mushed that bitch out of my way. Instantly, J-Money and Totta were at my side—pulling me backwards. I noticed the broad was talking mad shit as she pointed at me. Not giving two fucks about being in the club, I lifted my shirt and mouthed, "You can get domed down, bitch."

With my comment, she fled as Totta and J-Money pushed me towards the entrance of the club. Knowing that it was time for me to go, I stopped them niggas and told them not until I finished my bottles.

Totta yelped in my ears, "Fuck them bottles, nigga. You ain't right in the head. So, I'm finna take you home."

Seeing the bitch and her crew going to the security, I started laughing. Several moments later, The Savage Clique rolled up on us. X stepped in front of me, leaned closer towards me, and said,

"You aren't a part of my clique, but my niggas fucks with you heavy. So, I gotta step in before you do some crazy shit because of love. Let me treat you to some food, and you can vent to me. I'm not sure if I can help you or not, but I can ensure that I will listen to you."

Knowing that I couldn't refuse her invite, I nodded my head and walked behind her. Giving that she had major clout, I knew that no one would say anything about the alcohol I carried out the door. Hopping in the front seat of The Beast, as X demanded, she brought her whip to life. Leaning the seat back as she reversed her vehicle, X began talking to me and I listened. The difference between me listening to her versus to Totta, was that she commanded respect and for those to listen to her, and if they didn't, her punishments were hell to pay.

The entire drive to whatever restaurant she was going to, she talked. She touched on her personal experiences with love, and how badly she wanted it. She went so far as to tell me that she was giving up the throne so that she could pursue love and a fairy tale ending with the baby she was pregnant with. Everything she told me, I took to heart. I also saw the silver lining in the things that happened between Jonsey and me, and what The Savage Clique did for me tonight.

"Call her, Dank, and talk calmly to her. One thing I am trying to learn is that you never act out when you are dealing with your emotions. You'll never be able to control the situation. I know I'm the last one to talk, but of course, I pay people and I mean people to take care of my aftermath."

"I don't know what to say to her. I don't want her to say anything like she did the other night in front of people," I stated as X jumped on the Interstate.

"Simply tell her how you feel. I wished I had of done that with one person in particular," her soft voice spoke.

"Okay," I responded, not sure if I was going to do it.

"Do you have any questions?"

"Not at the moment I don't," I replied as I looked at the beautiful queen pin.

"Are you sure?" she chuckled.

"Nope," I laughed before asking, "You aren't as bad as people make you out to be."

"No, I'm not. Actually, I'm the sweetest person you'll ever meet. But fuck with my dope, my feelings, my crew, and money and see how fast Spot will motherfucking act up."

As we laughed at her comment, I shook my head. Time went by before we said another word. It was me who offered words first.

"X, thank you for talking to me tonight. I really needed to hear what you had to say. A nigga all messed up off the choices I decided to make. Now, I don't know which way to turn."

"No problem, Dank. Critical think on your situation. Whichever way you are leaning the heaviest on...go with that decision. Don't let your emotions tell you what you should do. Think Dank. You aren't dumb. I know what type of degrees and grades you made in school, so you are far from a dumb ass man."

With her last comment, she turned up her noise knockers and zoomed up the interstate. I had no damn idea where we were going, and I sure as hell wasn't going to ask. Why? Because I knew for certain that I hadn't pissed her or her goons off.

Keith Sweat "In the Rain" played as I did exactly what X suggested that I did—critical think. By the time she turned off on Exit 51 in Auburn, I had mentally put together the pros and cons of being with Jonsey. The pros outweighed the cons; yet, the biggest con was her comment the other night at my home. Based on that alone was the reason why I decided that I wasn't going to contact Jonsey; I couldn't afford for her to act that way again. I simply was going to let her be.

Chapter 19
Jonzella

Today was supposed to have been a loving day and joyful day; instead, it was pure hell and then some. I couldn't enjoy any of the nice things Totta did for me because I kept thinking about what Jonsey said she overheard. Even when I became horny and tried to molest Totta, I was still thinking about what my father had done to our brothers. I wanted to ask him about it, but a part of me told me to leave it alone. Truth be told, I didn't know if I should trust my father if he would do such a heartless act. I had so many unanswered questions that I began to answer them. I wanted to know was our mom involved, and if she was, I knew that she didn't need to know about my pregnancy. Speaking of my pregnancy, when Dad learned of it he was cooler than a fan. I expected for him to spaz out. He surely was stern when Kyvin mentioned that I could be. So, calling and confronting Dad about the conversation that Jonsey heard was not on my to-do list.

"What are you thinking about?" Totta inquired as he stepped into my room, looking like an entire Christmas meal.

"The ordeal Jonsey told us," I huffed as I lay on my back, staring at the ceiling.

"Care to elaborate," he voiced as he sat on the bed, facing me.

"Just wondering how in the hell am I supposed to be around him and Mom. I don't know who to trust. They were hell bent on us not getting pregnant, and here I am with a swollen uterus. Dad was very stern when Kyvin brought it up. Then, when I told him, he was okay with it. Now, I must think whether he is trying to sabotage my child's life," I told him truthfully as I placed my eyes on him.

"One thing I can promise you, Jonzella, is that no one is going to harm y'all and I mean that. My child and you mean the world to me. I'll lay it down for ours. I don't know what to tell you other than to be careful around them."

Sighing heavily, I leaned up and said, "I gotta check on Jonsey. She cried herself to sleep."

"Okay," he replied as he laid back on the bed.

"I'm surprised you aren't hitting the streets today," I stated as I climbed off the bed.

"Not in the mood for that honestly. Just wanna lay under you."

"So, is somebody trying to come out of the streets?" I inquired with a raised eyebrow.

"Yeah. I got a little one on the way, and he don't need to be brought into that lifestyle. Maybe you can help me decide on a legit career," he voiced seriously as he glared into my eyes.

With a smirk on my face, I said, "*He*? Who said anything about the baby being a he?"

Chuckling, Totta replied, "Out of all the shit I said...you focusing on the sex of the baby?"

"Yep," I snickered.

"Go check on your sister, and then we can argue about the gender of the baby later," he commanded while laughing and shaking his head.

Skipping out of my room, I took several deep breaths before approaching Jonsey's room. The moment I knocked on her door, her cell phone began ringing. With a racing heart, I wondered who was calling her. As she answered her phone, I was closing her door.

With a drunken face, she stared at the phone before saying, "It's daddy calling."

"Answer the phone and act normal," I replied as I ran to her bed, followed by getting in.

Doing as I commanded, Jonsey was a shaking mess. As she placed the call on speakerphone, my heart began to race.

"Hi, sweetheart. How are you and Jonzella?" our father said calmly.

"Good. How are you and mom?" Jonsey voiced before yawning.

"We are okay."

"That's good," she replied as she looked at me and mouthed what do I say.

"Jonsey?"

"Yes, sir?" she responded in a shaky tone.

"What did you overhear yesterday?" our father asked sternly.

"What are you talking about, Daddy? I didn't talk to you yesterday," she sighed, playing dumb—which I didn't think she could pull off, but she did.

"Don't play dumb with me, little girl. I know you were on my phone for twenty-five minutes...so, I'm going to ask you one more time...what did you hear?" he voiced in an annoyed timbre.

"Nothing," she replied in a scared timbre.

"Good, and make sure you keep it that way. There are things that you don't know and will never need to know...make sure you keep telling yourself that you heard nothing. Just know that Daddy had to do what he had to do," he voiced harshly at the same time my mouth flew open. I was beyond livid at my father's behavior and tone towards Jonsey.

"Yes, sir," Jonsey stated as tears seeped down her face.

Shaking my head, I took Jonsey's phone and wanted to tell him some things, but I knew that wasn't the best thing for me to do. Handing her phone back, I mouthed for her to get off the phone with him.

Nodding her head, Jonsey said, "Dad, I gotta go. My class is about to start. Tell Mom that I love her."

Chuckling, Dad responded, "You are not a good liar, dear. I know like hell you aren't in school. Anyways, tell your mother yourself that you love her."

Pushed to the point of no return, I boldly stated, "Should we be scared of you, Dad?"

"Indeed. Especially when you do foolish shit to make me look bad or make me spend unnecessary money...bringing unwanted heat my way."

The way our father spoke caused me to believe that he was involved in the street life. Knowing that anything was possible, I bit down on my bottom lip and lowly asked, "Are you about that life?"

Our father chuckled before replying, "Since I was thirteen."

With our mouths open, Jonsey and I glared at each other before mouthing, wow.

"Dad, it's not me if I don't ask this, but are you genuinely okay with me being pregnant? Are you going to come after me and my baby?"

Sighing heavily, our father said, "Yes, I'm okay with you being pregnant. You are grown, responsible, and very intelligent. You and Jonsey have never done anything to disappoint me to the point that I—"

Caught Up In A D-Boy's Illest Love 2

Letting his sentence linger in the air, the room was filled with silence. As my eyes were on Jonsey's blue and red covers, our father's voice boomed through the phone, causing me to jump.

"I don't expect y'all to look at me no different. Just know that I love y'all with every breath in me."

"You said the same thing about Kenny and Kevin. You fucked up my love life because of your bullshit. You sic'd that bitch nigga, Demante Wilks, on me and had the nerve to punish me because of loving him. For what? So, that you can do whatever you want illegal? All that shit you preached about doing right and staying away from the wrong crowd was a crock of shit, huh? So, you tell me how in the fuck I'm supposed to look at you and Mom after this shit? I don't trust neither of you!" Jonsey spat nastily as she wiped her tears away.

With a raised eyebrow and rapidly beating heart, I was astonished at my sister's comment. I wanted to tell her to calm down, but I couldn't. She went through a rough time with that Demante Wilks guy, and to hear that Father had something to do with it--had me shaking my head. I was loss for words as I took a quick trip down memory lane during the Jonsey and Demante era. She was one naïve and thrown off individual. No one could tell her that Demante wasn't about shit; other than a local jackboy mixed in with a drug dealer.

"I'm still your father and you better watch your tone when talking to me, dammit. Everything I've done and did was for a reason. You don't know everything, little girl, and that's for a reason. I'm going to say this once and once only...don't speak on shit that you don't know about. If I get a whiff of y'all running your damn mouths, let's just say the outcome won't be pretty," he voiced before ending the call.

Quickly staring at the screen, Jonsey and I held eye contact well over two minutes. Handing my sister back her phone, I had a thousand questions for her, and only one would question had to be asked so that I can be completely in the loop.

"In order for Daddy to speak the way he did, Jonsey, what all did you hear?"

Sighing sharply, she spoke, "Dad wanted devices him and Demante used to chat. Dad didn't have the $3000 to pay, which Dad didn't give him a deposit. He's paying fuck boy with the life insurance policies from Kevin and Kenny. Then Demante asked about me. Dad told him don't fuck with him. So, Demante hollered that he knew exactly where we lived thanks to Kevin and Kenny and that he wouldn't mind coming to pay my pussy a visit. Since I was his first...I highly believe that was a threat. The call ended after Demante called dad OG Brown."

"Oh my God," I quickly stated while shaking my head.

"I'm done with this shit. I'm disowning him. I don't know Mom's position, so I'm disowning her ass also. This is too much for me. All I know is that I'm finna start visiting the gun range and purchase me a couple of guns. I'm on high alert with our parents."

"Kyvin's ass might be next. Since, he likes men, and Daddy really ain't having it," I blurted out.

"I know I won't be on his damn list. We need to be looking at a new place to live," she replied seriously as she rubbed her forehead.

Ding. Ding.

Picking up her phone, she unlocked it. Staring at the app My Period Tracker, it informed her that she was five days late.

With wide eyes, I laughed, "Well, damn."

"I don't have time for this shit!" she yelled as she threw her phone on the floor.

"Girl, you know your period is crazy once you are stressed. So, calm down, and the motherfucker will be on. Now, if you want to take a test, then I have an extra one," I told her softly.

Looking at me crazily, she spat, "Why do you have one? You already know you knocked up."

"Because I bought two just in case I messed up on the first one," I told her as I hopped off the bed, aiming for the door.

"Go get it, so I can calm my nerves. Between Casey and Daddy's bullshit, I'm about to go postal," she huffed before jumping off the bed.

"Okay," I stated before leaving her room.

As I strolled along, I prayed that Jonsey wasn't pregnant. She wasn't ready for motherhood. Her being pregnant would break her more than make her. She wasn't strong-willed like me; she would be on a level that I wouldn't be able to tolerate. She was going to turn into the female that she was while dating Demante and that was extremely unhealthy for her. If she was pregnant, I was surely going to suggest that she got an abortion.

"How's Jonsey doing?" Totta asked as he flipped the channels on the TV.

Not knowing how to answer his question, I replied, "I really don't know."

Grabbing the pregnancy test from my first drawer, Totta said, "Wait a whole damn minute—"

"Shut yo' ass up, and you bet not say shit to Casey either. You stay out of their business as I'm trying to do," I announced sternly, ensuring that my eyes were planted on him.

"Okay," he replied obediently as he licked his lips.

"Soon as I make sure she don't set this duplex on fire, I will be back to put something on those lips," I voiced naughtily.

"Hurry back then!" he shouted before chuckling and rubbing on his dick.

Damn near running out of the room, I almost bumped into Jonsey. Handing her the pregnancy test, we entered the bathroom. With my nerves on end, I began praying hard that the test only had one line. As my sister opened the box, she was talking mad shit. Thus, I prayed harder! Sitting on the toilet, she peed on the stick. My heart almost ran out of my chest; I had to do breathing exercises so that I wouldn't raise my pressure.

Placing the test on the counter, she said, "It better have one line, or it's going to be some flames in the city today!"

"Jonsey, please calm down. You know we've had a scare when you were dating Demante, and it was just your stress level," I spat calmly before I thought, *Father, God, please don't let this test have two lines. You know what type of person Jonsey is, and I can't manage her and my pregnancy without losing my child or mind.*

After wiping and washing her hands, we heard her phone ringing. Leaving the bathroom to retrieve her phone, I looked at the test and damn near fainted.

"God, help me," I replied lowly as I shook my head.

Coming into the bathroom with a frown on her face, Jonsey said, "Who in the fuck is this?"

The look on her face told me who it was. Immediately, I put the toilet seat down followed by sitting on it. As my sister went off on

Demante, I shook my head. I cursed out my father and her. The shit they were putting me through was too much. Soon as she hung up the phone, tears were streaming down her face. Seeing how she went through two emotions, anger and fearful, in a matter of seconds, I knew I was going to need four blunts and six bottles of Patron after dealing with her today. The fucked-up part was that I couldn't have any of it. So, I had to deal with Jonsey sober! I was not a happy camper. I continued to ask myself why in the hell was she so fucking careless when she knew that she shouldn't have been!

Throwing the phone into her room, Jonsey aggressively asked, "What did it say?"

"Two lines," I replied casually as I shook my head.

The moment I said that, Jonsey flew to the counter, picked up the test, and glared at the test. She didn't say anything just breathed heavily all the while biting down on her bottom lip.

Sighing heavily, I calmly demanded, "Jonsey, don't do anything that will make you look stupid. Please, don't act out of character, and please, please, think rationally before you do and say anything crazy. If you want to have an abortion, I'm with you one-hundred percent, and I won't look at you no different."

"Girl, fuck an abortion. He got his wish...for me to be in the same position you are. I am...so, he better get with the program, or he ain't gon' have one peaceful night in this motherfucking city," she stated calmly while staring into my eyes.

"Well, the crazy bitch is back and in full effect," I mumbled as I watched my sister plop down on her bed with her phone in her hand.

Chapter 20
Totta

Wednesday, February 15th

"Aye, Danzo, do you remember saying something about the girls' parents having something to do with those fuck boys' death?" I asked him as him, Dank, and I chilled at my crib playing Madden 2016.

"Yep," he replied as he sloppily chewed on a pulled pork sandwich.

Agitated at the way he ate, I said, "Woe, will you please stop eating like a damn Billy goat. The shit is super annoying."

With Dank laughing, it caused Danzo to keep chewing, further pissing me off.

"After you answer my question, please get the fuck out my crib," I spat in an annoyed timbre.

Smacking his nasty mouth, Danzo replied with, "I told you I saw some suspicious shit on them folks' computer. I couldn't further investigate because I heard several voices coming down the hallway. I know I saw three web pages up about some type of medicine, head trauma, and State Farm. Why? What's up?"

"The daddy confessed to having the boys killed. Well, someone overheard the conversation. I need the daddy and momma looked closely into," I voiced to him.

Nodding his head, he replied, "Where are we starting at first?"

"The Savage Clique," I replied as I looked amongst him and Dank.

Both nodding their heads, I knew that I had to reach out to J-Money, soon as the betted video game ended.

As Dank and I made a smooth transition into the second quarter of the game, he asked, "How's the ladies doing?"

"My queen good, and Jonsey all over the place," I told him, trying my best to keep my mouth shut about her pregnancy.

"What's wrong with her?" he inquired as he briefly looked at me.

"Dealing with family and your issues. Maybe you should call and talk to her," I suggested.

"Nawl, I'mma leave her alone. I can't take no chances of her blowing up like she did, mane. I'll just keep getting updates from you, whenever I ask," he quickly voiced before continuing. "I'm just hoping she ain't gon' hit a nigga up talking about she pregnant. That shit there would be catastrophic."

Well, woe, get ready for that phone call, I thought as I was surprised that she hadn't called and told him about her news.

"What you do if she is?" Danzo asked, beating me to the punch.

"Honestly, I don't even know. All I know is that I gotta stir clear of her. It's the best thing at this point," he voiced before exhaling.

"But she knows that we didn't harm her brothers, even though, we were trying," I told him.

"If they get in another heated argument, she might mention that shit," Danzo voiced as he lay back on the sofa.

Dank pointed at Danzo and said, "What that nigga said."

Sighing heavily, I was at a crossroads. I wanted to tell him that Jonsey was pregnant, but I kept hearing my queen's voice saying that I better not say shit. Knowing that Dank and I go way back since we were teens, I had to say something.

"Woe, I got some shit to tell you," I huffed as I paused the game.

"What?" they asked in unison.

"Not you, Danzo, but Dank...this for you. I hate to be the one say this but umm... Jonsey is pregnant. She pissed on a stick yesterday."

While Danzo stupid ass started laughing, Dank was shaking his head. As my partner kept his eyes on me, he didn't say anything. Niggas glared in my face with the 'I know you lying' face. Moments passed before he spoke.

"Woe, I ain't saying shit until she do," he replied before telling me to unpause the game.

Analyzing Dank before I entertained the game, I was shocked as hell to know that he wasn't on the phone with Jonsey. Not about to have him in the deadbeat dad zone, I had to know what was up.

"Mane, you been nutting in that girl, and you gon' sit up here like you ain't caring about nothing that I said."

"Shid, I ain't finna run behind no damn body that can potentially have them folks looking at me. I can't deal with her possible outbursts. A nigga ain't got time to be on pins and needles when in an argument with Jonsey. So, if she don't tell me, I'm cool with that. If she do, then shid...her and I gotta have a long talk. She gon' know why a nigga can't be with her."

Hearing the most absurd statement ever produced out of Dank's mouth, I shook my head and unpaused the game. It was his personal life, and I was going to stay the fuck out it. Once the game was over with, I hopped on the phone with J-Money. I told him what I needed, and he asked for a further alliance within The Savage Clique. With him knowing that I wanted to come out of the street life, he and I proposed that we sit down and discuss things further. By the end of our conversation, I knew the perfect way of paying him back for helping me learning the truth about my queen's father. I was going to go legit in a field that The Savage Clique can benefit from!

Twenty-three minutes after I ended the call with J-Money, Dank and Danzo left my crib. I wasn't far behind them as I was on a mission to see what my momma was preparing for dinner. Wednesdays were her off days; those days she cooked heavy.

Pulling into her yard, I saw her sitting on the porch, smoking a cigarette, and bobbing her head.

Stepping out of the car, I said, "Hey, woman. How's your day?"

"Good, son, good. How's your day, and how's Jonzella doing?" she asked sweetly.

"My day a'ight, and she's doing great," I smiled as I bent low to give her a hug.

Observing me, my mother glared into my face. Pondering why she was analyzing me so, I had to ask.

"Why are you looking at me like that, Ma?"

"Since, Jonzella said that she was pregnant, you have been different. What are your plans, son?"

"Going legit, doing the right thing by our child and her," I said truthfully.

With a smile on her face, my mother said, "I'm so glad that she brings out the best in you. I'm tired of praying heavily that you will leave the streets alone and that I don't get one of those midnight calls. The streets are treacherous, son, as I'm sure you know."

Nodding my head, I replied, "I know. The main reason I know it's time to give it up. I will have two people depending on me to be alive and free, and a brother is going to take full advantage of that."

As we chatted and laughed, I felt at peace about leaving the streets. I did some cruel things while slanging meth; yet, I had to do it in order to survive the crumb ducklings of the street life. True enough, I had no business entertaining that life with a full scholarship to college playing baseball; however, like my partner, Dank, I jumped in just to have some shit to do. Growing up, I never wanted for anything—love, attention, or materialistic things. Momma made sure we, including her, never went without! She's been an RN since she had my eldest sister.

By the time one of her jams played at a nice decibel, I walked inside to use the bathroom. As I drained my man, my phone chimed. After I handled my business, I pulled my cell phone out and read the text from my queen.

Bae: *Just wanted to let you know that I love you and I'm thinking about you.*

With a huge smile on my face, I replied.

Me: *I love you more girl.*

"Totta!" my mother yelled.

"Yes!" I hollered as I shoved my phone in my pocket as I turned on the water knob.

"Come here!" she yelled.

Wondering why in the hell she was yelling like that, I asked the moment I opened the bathroom door. Strolling down the hallway, I had to think whether I ate her cookies and hadn't replaced them. A ninja didn't have time to be running around the neighborhood behind them damn cookies! Approaching the screen door, I had a mean mug on my face.

Pressing the black handle on the screen door, I said, "What's up, Momma?"

Before she got a chance to speak, a short, bald-headed police officer said, "Joshua Nixon, we would like for you to come downtown with us."

"What for?" my mother asked aggressively while standing.

Before I got the chance to say the one word that I knew well, lawyer, the short officer said, "He's wanted for questioning in the involvement of Erica Lickson's endangerment."

Fuck the bitch is still alive, I thought as I looked at my mother and said, "Lawyer." ....

About the Novelist

TN Jones was born and raised Alabama. She currently resides in her native state with her boyfriend and their daughter. Growing up, TN Jones always had a passion for reading and writing. She began writing short stories when she was a young. As a college student, TN Jones enjoyed writing academic research papers, which heightened her passion for writing.

After a bilateral axilla and inguinal surgery in 2015, she started working on her first book, *Disloyal: Revenge of a Broken Heart*. TN Jones will write in the following genres: Contemporary Fiction, Urban Fiction, Mystery/Suspense, Interracial/Urban Romance, Dark Erotica, Paranormal, and Fantasy Fiction.

Published novels by TN Jones: *Disloyal: Revenge of a Broken Heart, Disloyal 2: A Woman's Revenge, Disloyal 3: A Woman's Revenge, A Sucka in Love for a Thug, If You'll Give Me Your Heart 1-2, By Any Means: Going Against the Grain 1-2, The Sins of Love: Finessing the Enemies 1 & 2, and Caught Up in a D-Boy's Illest Love 1.*

Upcoming books by TN Jones: *The Sins of Love 3: Finessing the Enemies and Choosing To Love A Lady Thug series.*

Caught Up In A D-Boy's Illest Love 2

Thank you for reading the second installment of *Caught Up In A D-Boy's Illest Love*. Please leave an honest review under the book title on Amazon's page.

For future book details, please visit any of the following links:

Amazon Author page: https://www.amazon.com/tnjones666

Facebook: https://www.facebook.com/novelisttnjones/

Goodreads:
https://www.goodreads.com/author/show/14918893.TN_Jones:

Google+:
https://www.plus.google.com/u/1/communities/115057649956960897339

Instagram: https://www.instagram.com/tnjones666

Twitter: https://twitter.com/TNHarris6.

You are welcome to email her: tnjones666@gmail.com; as well as chat with her daily in the Facebook group, **It's Just Me...TN Jones**.

CPSIA information can be obtained
at www.ICGtesting.com
Printed in the USA
LVHW091742191219
641092LV00002B/333/P